198 Pages

LAZARUS LONGMAN
CHRONICLES

  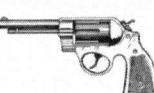

GOLDEN HEART

P. J. Thorndyke

LONDON

Number 1   1885

Golden Heart
By P. J. Thorndyke

2020 by Copyright © P. J. Thorndyke

All rights reserved. This book or any portion thereof may not be reproduced or used in any manner whatsoever without the express written permission of the publisher except for the use of brief quotations in a book review.

Contents

Chapter One 1
Chapter Two 13
Chapter Three 21
Chapter Four 33
Chapter Five 45
Chapter Six 57
Chapter Seven 73
Chapter Eight 83
Chapter Nine 97
Chapter Ten 107
Chapter Eleven 119
Chapter Twelve 127
Chapter Thirteen 139
Chapter Fourteen 153
Chapter Fifteen 167
Chapter Sixteen 175
Chapter Seventeen 187

Chapter Eighteen 195
A Note from the Author 205
Sneak Peek - Silver Tomb 207

Chapter One

In which our hero takes a cold dip in the Colorado River

Perhaps the most disreputable den of thieves, murderers, hustlers and gamblers in either the Confederate or United States of America is not in some seedy boomtown or frontier outpost, but on water. If the above description had to be applied to any establishment, then just about every individual in the Southwest, be they gold digger, hat salesman or dirigible engineer, would undoubtedly name the *Mary Sue*.

The golden age of the paddle steamer enjoyed its heyday during the early years of the American war. With the construction of the Southern Pacific Railroad that bridged the Colorado River, the luxurious steamers fell into the hands of private entrepreneurs. Like many of her sister vessels, the crisp white paint of the *Mary Sue* had curled and faded to a filthy grey, her sleek black funnels rusted to a rough brown and the massive paddles on either side turned green with scum and algae.

The owner of the *Mary Sue* was a villain named Steve McCluskey, or 'Steamboat Steve' as he was fondly known by his patrons. He had won the *Mary Sue* in a poker game and turned it into a floating pleasure palace of the very worst kind. Its ballrooms and restaurants became casinos and sawdust-saloons, and its lower decks dimly lit bordellos. It became notorious for its rough clientele who wished to enjoy themselves far from the eyes of the authorities, and the Colorado River was a winding, treacherous vein between the Unionist north and the Confederate south that no man could lay claim to.

Lazarus Longman looked around at what had once been a fabulous ballroom. Beneath the grimy film of nicotine that coated the ceiling, he could make out the cherubs tootling on their little trumpets as they gazed down on the crowd through the dully twinkling glass of the chandelier, no doubt with distaste at the drastic change in clientele the last few years had seen. Several other original features remained like the marble bar top and brass rail, now cracked and unpolished.

The great paddles thrummed to the blaze of the furnace from the engine room, but the noise was barely noticeable in the casino as it was drowned out by the racket from the tables and the bar. Lazarus watched the bartender take his empty glass and toss the dregs and lemon slice into a copper bin before refilling it with gin and tonic water, topping it off with a fresh lemon slice and sliding it back to him across the bar.

He turned and scanned the room, taking in characteristics and mentally ticking them off his checklist. He wasn't too sure what his quarry looked like, having nothing to go on but a rather fudgy wanted poster, prints of which could be seen in every railway station, dirigible dock, town and trading post in the Southwest. So far, he had narrowed the possibilities down to three. One was a surly fellow who laid down chips like they were going out of fashion. Another was a heavy drinker who kept the bar wet with the whiskey that missed his mouth. The third seemed to mix the two pursuits, spilling whiskey on the green felt of the poker table. All had something resembling the unshaven, scarred visage of the infamous bandit.

One of Steamboat Steve's security measures was that all passengers had to turn in their artillery upon boarding. The high stakes at the gaming tables, and the explosive nature of the clientele made this a must, even for somebody with such a liberal philosophy as Steve McCluskey. But looking around at the scarred faces, missing ears and what could only be described as a 'colorful' palette around him, Lazarus sorely felt the emptiness of the holster that usually held his British Enfield Mk II under his left armpit. But he took some comfort in the reassuring lump in his right boot signifying a hidden Colt London Pocket. Fortunately, they hadn't checked him too thoroughly, although he had to wonder how thoroughly they had checked his fellow passengers.

There were a few other characters he was watching too, but merely out of curiosity. One was the gorilla-sized ruffian at the entrance whom he took to be one of Steamboat Steve's hired guns. The bulge under his jacket was the giveaway. The other was a woman. The presence of a woman was certainly not uncommon on the *Mary Sue*, however the presence of a woman who was not a whore was unique. In fact, she was the only woman in the casino; the stable of mechanized whores McCluskey owned were strictly confined below decks.

This was the norm for all such establishments. Mechanicals were a slave class and since the passing of the Emancipation Act they had replaced black people on the lowest rung of society's ladder, barred from public accommodation and most private establishments.

She wore a nicely-fitting red and black corset with a low, square neckline and sleeves trimmed with black lace. A small black hat was perched on the front of her head. Her hair was dark and her skin pale with petite yet severe features. She stood on one of the raised sections of the room with a glass of what looked like gin in one gloved hand. The other hand rested lightly on the brass railing. Lazarus could see that she was scanning the room, as he was, looking for somebody—a lover? He stopped to wonder why he was letting this distract him from his task.

One of the three candidates—the surly gambler—had left the poker table in sullen silence at having run out of chips and made his way over to the bar, looking like he was on the verge of tears. Lazarus immediately scratched him off the list.

Two to go.

The drinker had finally reached his limit and lay slumped over the bar, inert. Far too drunk for a wanted bandit to allow himself to become in a public place. He looked over at the third candidate, who suddenly let out a yell of triumph at winning a game and stood up, raising his glass. "Here's to the *Mary Sue*, the finest goddamn whore I ever rode!"

Bingo.

Gerard Vasquez was of French-Mexican descent. He had been a captain in the Confederate Dirigible Corps but for unknown reasons had absconded with one of their smaller vessels, along with a gigantic Navajo called Hok'ee who had enough mechanical implants to be considered less than human by many. The pair were like blood brothers for some reason and had been living the lives of pirates; committing bank robberies, raids and kidnappings throughout the Southwest, striking from their airship which Vasquez had renamed the *Santa Bella*. The Confederate government had tried to shoot them down on numerous occasions without success.

The roar of appreciation at Vasquez's joke died down and play resumed at the tables. Confident that his quarry was going nowhere for the foreseeable future, Lazarus decided to take the air on deck. The matter that had brought him on board the *Mary Sue* was far too delicate to attempt in the casino. He would have to invite the bandit for a private drink later on.

The cool breeze of the Colorado River was refreshing. Lazarus lit a cigarette and tossed the match overboard. He watched the black shapes of the mountains and desert plateaus slide past. It had taken him days to track Vasquez to the *Mary Sue*. His government wanted the bandit turned over to the Confederates alive, and tonight was the night he would finally accomplish his mission and begin the long voyage home.

Home to London.

It had been over a year since he had trod the cobbled streets of that city. It was no lie that he missed the sounds and smells of those crowded warrens with their stalls and shops, hawkers and whores who sold their wares in the shadow of St. Paul's dome.

His months in the Americas had been long and life changing. He should have returned home sooner but he hadn't had the heart. After what had happened in South America he had just wanted to disappear. He didn't feel like himself anymore. He didn't know his place in the grand scheme of things, if ever there was some divine plan with which all humanity must comply. So, he had journeyed north, hoping to find some place to die quietly with a bottle of something strong in his hand. But as Whitehall's only man in the Confederate States, he had been the prime candidate for this new mission and somehow, they had tracked him down.

Handing Vasquez over was his only objective. Lazarus had made sure that had been clear. He was not a hired gun or a bounty hunter. In truth, he was a historian and an archeologist, much more at home in the library than pursuing the political ambitions of Her Majesty's government. Vasquez knew something. And it was Lazarus's job to ensure the Confederate government had the chance to pry it out of him.

Once he had done that, he could return home to try and find his place again. He had an unfinished manuscript on the ruins of Great Zimbabwe on his desk and notes for his second series of lectures on the Valley of the Kings. The time for digging around in dusty tombs and fighting through steaming jungles was over. It was time to return to an academic existence. But it was an ironic fact of his life that the subjects of his books and lectures frequently got in the way of the writing of them.

His train of thought was interrupted when his glance fell upon the footprint on the deck. It was large, boot-shaped and wet. It was one of a series, growing fainter and drier the further they got from the rail, eventually disappearing. It hadn't been raining.

Lazarus wandered back to the casino and did a quick head count. There were several newcomers—heavy, thick-set characters wearing dusters. They had spread out and had all the exits covered, some on the gaming floor and some on the raised sections. McCluskey's hired goon was none the wiser. Lazarus edged closer to the foot of a raised section and peered through the railings at the boots of the nearest thug. They were wet, as was the hem of his duster.

Lazarus looked about for the woman in red and black but could not see her. Strange that she should have disappeared at this exact moment. He cursed his distracted mind, for one of the thugs had drawn a sawn-off shotgun and raised it into the air. He just had time to drop to one knee and thrust his hand into his right boot as the shot went off, a deafening roar tearing apart the fun in the casino and peppering the cherubs in the ceiling with buckshot.

McCluskey's goon went for his gun and was sent hurtling over the railing by a blast from behind, his ruptured innards spattering the nearest poker table and its players. The barman ducked behind the counter and emerged with his own shotgun but didn't get a chance to fire a round as one from another gun took him apart, sending him crashing into the mirror behind the bar, shattering glass and bottles. It happened so fast that those in the crowd who had concealed firearms barely had a chance to draw them.

"Nobody else move, goddammit!" cried the thug in the centre of the room. "We ain't here to rob you! We just want to relieve you of a very nasty and disreputable man by the name of Gerard Vasquez!"

Damn! thought Lazarus, feeling around in his boot for the butt of his Colt London. *Bounty Hunters.*

"Step right up Mr. Vasquez and come with us!" the gunman continued. "No need to be shy!"

Lazarus looked to Vasquez who sat calmly toying with his hand of cards, his other hand hidden beneath the table. Lazarus was not concerned that his quarry might end up in the hands of these goons. Vasquez was too good for that. But a stray bullet might put an end to him before Lazarus could spirit him away. He had to do something, and fast.

Time was up and Vasquez was on his feet in an instant, hurling the card table over, his LeMat revolver spitting fire in the direction of the lead bounty hunter. And that was when, as they say, all hell broke loose. Those whose twitching fingers had been hovering over the straps and bulges that hid their weapons now broke them free and picked their targets.

Several of the passengers were dead almost instantaneously, their final hand played out and their blood running in rivulets along the wooden planks. Lazarus rose and drew his pistol, dropping one of the bounty hunters in a heartbeat. He dived behind a faux-Georgian pillar as the deadly volley of vengeance headed his way. The exits were still blocked. Vasquez kept his head low as shotgun blasts slowly ate away at his cover in showers of splinters and clouds of green felt.

"To your left, Vasquez!" Lazarus cried, poking his head around the pillar. "Make for the door. I'll cover you!"

The bandit did not hesitate to find out who his sudden ally was and they moved together in synchronism; Vasquez running for the door in a hunched over position, and Lazarus blasting at each of the intruders in turn, keeping their attention fixed solely on him.

He saw Vasquez vanish. Now it was time for him to make his move. Two of the gunmen had followed the bandit out and the others were occupying themselves with hurling their anger at Lazarus, blast after blast crunching through the pillar and biting deep into the wood.

He heard the sound of a shotgun being broken so that a greasy thumb could slide in more cartridges. Rolling from behind the pillar, he fired once, shattering the face of one of the gunmen. In a maelstrom of pellets and wooden splinters, he made for the door.

Out on deck he came across the bodies of two bounty hunters lying in pools of blood. One, which was pierced by a medium caliber, had undoubtedly been struck by Vasquez's return fire but the other had a hole in its chest the size of a cannonball, which greatly unnerved Lazarus.

His feet pounded wooden planking as he chased after his quarry, swinging around a banister and leaping down the stairs that led below decks. The corridors were dim, lit only by the red of the fringed fabric wall lamps. There was the occasional green gas light above a door, signifying that it was unoccupied. Lazarus could see the silhouette of Vasquez ahead of him, making for the exit on the other side of the steamer.

There was a deafening roar. Lazarus recognized the sound of a Golgotha rifle and knew to duck as the round passed over his head. He spun around and fired, immediately knowing that it was useless. McCluskey's more expensive security measure had caught up with them.

The Mecha-guard fired off another round, its right arm that tapered into the point of the rifle blazing orange in the dimness. These mechanized guards were heavy duty soldiers; organic matter encased in metal. Its furnace blazed purple, and steam hissed from the funnel on its left shoulder. Lazarus could make out the oily rivets and plate iron and knew that his petty weapon would have no effect.

As he fled, he could hear old Steamboat Steve screeching from behind. "Go on you great lug! Gettem!"

Lazarus brushed past a half-naked customer who had scampered out of one of the rooms in a state of terror, hopping about with his britches half falling off.

"Hey," the Mecha-whore cried behind him, shambling out into the corridor. "You did not insert a coin into the slot! Please insert coin!"

The blast from the Mecha-guard's rifle caught her in the middle, sending shards of razor-edged metal thudding into the paneled walls. The Mecha-whore turned around in surprise and caught a second round in the chest. Chunks of organic matter splattered everywhere. McCluskey howled.

"Don't shoot the whores, goddamit! They cost a fortune to repair, not to mention replacing the organic!"

Lazarus made it to the other side of the steamer in one piece and caught up with Vasquez. He pointed his pistol at him. Vasquez eyed him suspiciously.

"You ain't one of them," the bandit said. "Who are you?

"Somebody who wants you alive," Lazarus said.

Vasquez's eyes glared at the gun barrel. "Funny way of showing it."

Another rifle blast tore through the railings and they both took cover behind some packing crates. The

Mecha-guard stomped out on deck and began searching for them, its organic pilot peering through slits in its iron helmet. It blasted apart a crate and Lazarus thanked his stars he wasn't behind it. But it wouldn't take long for it to find them.

Two shotgun blasts from behind the Mecha-guard were fired off in quick succession, knocking it forward. It turned around slowly, looking for its attacker. Lazarus peeped over the edge of his crate and saw the woman in red and black striding towards them, firing round after round from a shotgun with an automatic magazine, chomping away at the Mecha-guard's iron plating, pushing it back, back, towards the railings. A final blast sent it through the railings, and it tumbled down into the blades of the propeller.

There was a terrible sound of splintering wood and grinding metal. The great paddlewheel exploded, sending torn planks hurtling skywards as metal rims popped off at the sides. The steamer began to lurch and drift to starboard. Lazarus stood up to thank the woman for saving their bacon, and then ducked just in time to avoid being hit by another blast from her shotgun.

"Damn, woman! What have you got against me?"

"You are getting in my way," she replied in a strong Eastern European accent. "Where is Vasquez?"

"Who's askin'?" Vasquez said, rising slowly.

He got the same greeting Lazarus got, only lower. It missed him as well, tearing loose a chunk of the crate he was hiding behind. He fired back, but the woman swung behind a corner, all billowing skirts and shotgun smoke.

Lazarus saw Vasquez rise and hurry towards her position, gun held outwards. He got up and dashed towards him. Vasquez cried out a curse as he barreled into him, and they struck the railing as one. Loosened by the Mecha-guard's recent departure, the railing gave way. Lazarus just had time to catch a glimpse of the woman's enraged face above them before the water hit them like a sheet of glass.

Down, down they floundered, bubbles of air rushing up around them like fairy lights. By the time they rose to the surface, the *Mary Sue* was far downstream, its single remaining paddle turning it in slow circles. Gunshots cracked through the night air.

"Christ, you idiot!" Vasquez howled. "Why didn't you let me pop her?"

Lazarus didn't have an answer to that and struggled to keep a grip on his hostage, but the current was too strong and Vasquez managed to wriggle out of his grasp.

They drifted farther and farther apart. Lazarus could make out the shape of a small boat making its way towards them. Men in dusters stood aboard. Guns spoke out and Lazarus dived to avoid being hit. When he rose, he saw that the bounty hunters had apprehended Vasquez and were dragging him aboard their small vessel. He cursed and headed for shore.

Chapter Two

In which an appointment is kept in Yuma

Lazarus sat in the saloon that overlooked the railway depot and watched the mechanicals loading and unloading the trains. Steam drifted about the platforms, obscuring the gargantuan Athena-class locomotives as they sat cooling their engines. He sipped his IPA slowly and frowned as the door opened. A man walked in wearing a bowler hat and carrying a briefcase. He stood below the sign that read, 'No Mechanicals or Colored' for a bit before spotting Lazarus.

"I had hoped that I was missing in action," Lazarus said as the man came over to his table and drew up a chair.

"You're not all that devilish to find, you know," said the visitor in a voice that marked him out as another Englishman. He set his briefcase down and motioned to the bartender for another two pale ales.

"What are you doing here, Morton?" Lazarus asked. "There's nothing out here but warm beer, bandits and dust. Whores too, of course, although I suppose you aren't interested in them."

Morton frowned. "I'm here because we need this job finished."

"I can't do it. Vasquez is in the hands of the bounty hunters. I failed and I'm sorry."

"We need you to try again."

"Then get somebody else."

"And what are you going to do? Sit in here and drink yourself to death?"

"Actually, I thought I might return home. I've got plenty to occupy my time with back in England. I might write another book."

"Don't tell me you're going to start writing trashy fiction like Agent Haggard."

Lazarus had met Haggard in Africa, and it was through that particular English operative that he had been approached by Morton with an offer to work for the bureau. Haggard had indeed written a novel that closely mirrored their adventures in southern Africa, but the plot of the bestselling *King Solomon's Mines* had been altered enough for its author to avoid being hauled over the coals by Morton's bureau.

"I don't think I'm the novel-writing type," Lazarus said. "But I had great plans before I began working for you, Morton. There's still a few tomes in me on the subject of ancient civilizations."

"Yes, well there's one ancient civilization in particular that we're currently interested in," Morton replied.

"I keep telling you that it doesn't exist," Lazarus replied testily. "And I'm not your bloody bounty hunter."

Morton narrowed his eyes. "You're not swanning around Africa for the Royal Archaeological Institute now, old boy. You are whatever Whitehall says you are and what's more, you're *here*. And nobody else is. Can't you understand the importance of this?"

"Morton, you know I spent over a year up to my arse in yellow fever and irate natives in South America looking for El Dorado on your orders. All I found was a lake and a myth. And all I got for my efforts was blood on my hands." He took a gulp of beer, letting the sourness of it numb the sting in his throat.

"You know that I regret that whole business more than anybody, Longman…"

"Not more than I do. And not more than the people who lived on the shores of Lake Guatavita did. My point is that it will be the same story here. The natives made up these fantastical fairy tales like El Dorado and Cibola to keep the Spaniards on the trot. They didn't want those damned fellows making off with their women, so they kept telling them stories of golden cities and sunken treasures that were just over in the next valley. And the next. And the next. Not a bad scam, really," he added, sipping his beer thoughtfully.

"How can you be so cynical?" Morton said. "You—an archaeologist who has devoted his life to uncovering the secrets of antiquity."

"For God's sake, Morton, this isn't like the pyramids at Giza, or the ruins of Pompeii. There is simply no academic evidence to support its existence."

"Now, you know as well as I do that Cibola was mentioned by Cabeza De Vaca and Marcos De Niza..."

"Both of whom were Spaniards. It was all a swindle, Morton. The legend of seven golden cities was a Spanish bedtime story before Columbus ever got lost at sea. When America was found, they believed that it was the fabled land seven of their bishops had fled to following the Moorish invasion of Spain in the eighth century. The legend was that these seven bishops took all their wealth with them, and each established a city in this land across the ocean. The American natives either seized on this wishful thinking and exploited it, or by simple coincidence used the number seven in their own fairy tale for the conquistadores. When Coronado followed De Niza's footsteps, all he found were poor pueblos. Those are your cities of gold."

"De Niza claimed to have seen the golden cities from afar…" said Morton.

"No. He claimed to have seen Cibola but he mentioned nothing of gold. Either he deliberately misled everybody or they leapt to conclusions."

"But," continued Morton, not to be perturbed, "Gerard Vasquez is said to have seen a map of Cibola with his own eyes. An ancient map."

Lazarus rolled his eyes. He had heard all this before. Vasquez and his travelling companion Hok'ee had gone looking for Cibola themselves in their stolen dirigible. They had a map but had been unable to complete their search for reasons unknown. So they had hidden it. The Confederates wanted the map, and the British were more than willing to help them get it. If the gold could be found, then the stalemate between north and south could be ended. The Confederacy would take over the whole continent and become a powerful friend for the British.

"Chaps boast a lot when they drink as much as Vasquez does," said Lazarus in a tired voice. "This could all be pipe smoke."

"The President doesn't think so," said Morton. "And neither does Whitehall. We need Vasquez delivered into the government's hands. That's the only way this dreadful war can be brought to a close."

"By obliterating the other side with war-machines paid for by stolen gold."

"Don't be such a damned bleeding heart, Longman. Somebody's got to win."

"And we're backing the C.S.A."

"Britain needs the cotton. There's bother in Egypt as you've no doubt heard. General Gordon is fighting some mad Mohammedan and his dervishes in the Soudan as we speak, and the supply has currently dried up. And besides, by helping the C.S.A we might stand a chance at getting our hands on some of their mechanite. The United States certainly wouldn't let us get a look in. With a trade agreement between the C.S.A and Britain, we could become the greatest power in Europe. Bigger even than Russia."

Mechanite was the new big thing. Discovered in 1861 not long after the firing on Fort Sumter by the Confederacy, it had revolutionized the war. No mineral had ever been discovered that could match its efficiency. Originally found in California, veins had also been discovered in the southern states, and with both sides in possession of the energy source the war looked set to continue indefinitely. But the Americans guarded their mechanite jealously. Despite extensive mining operations in Europe, Africa and Asia, no sign of the valuable ore had turned up. It seemed like North America was the only spot on Earth blessed with the mineral and they weren't sharing, placing embargoes on it that made it exclusively a domestic commodity. The powers of Europe were in a desperate bid to gain access to America's deposits, but despite their wish for open European support, neither the U.S.A nor the C.S.A were willing to see their exclusive mineral become a commodity across the Atlantic.

"The only problem is that Vasquez is long gone, I'm afraid," said Lazarus.

"No," Morton replied. "He's here. In Yuma. His captors are planning on taking him aboard the 3:10 to

Great Salt Lake City."

"The State of Deseret? What do the Mormons want with him?"

"It was they who paid those bounty hunters to snatch him. He apparently committed a grievous series of crimes in Deseret. Their governor and president of their church want to hang him."

"I'd be tempted to let them."

"Get him, Longman. Its orders, I'm afraid. Once you have him, your best bet is to get him to Fort Flagstaff. There's a general there who's in the loop."

"I bloody well nearly froze to death in the Colorado River trying to get him two nights ago," Lazarus told him. "I lost my hat. I lost my gun. And it was a good gun. Given to me by General Wolseley in the Ashanti Campaign."

Morton lifted his briefcase onto the table and clipped it open. Shiny brass and polished iron glowed within. He lifted out a weapon and offered it butt-first to Lazarus. Lazarus took it.

"A Colt Starblazer..." he mumbled. "Are these available in London?"

"They're available to us," Morton replied with a knowing smile.

"My Enfield was inscribed..."

Morton drew out a second pistol. It was a snub and had a barrel about two inches in diameter with a wicked caliber. "This just came out of Belgium," he said, smiling at Lazarus's slack jaw. "The most powerful pistol about. It has explosive rounds."

"More powerful than a Golgotha?" Lazarus asked, feeling the hefty weight of the thing.

"Yes. And you can't hide a Golgotha in your boot. Now then, I believe that should be adequate firepower.

The train leaves tomorrow afternoon. Be ready. You won't be able to snatch him at the station, there will be too many of them, but once they are out on the open plains you should be able to get aboard with a fast horse. How you go about extracting him, I leave to you."

Lazarus considered mentioning the woman with the Eastern European accent who had thrown a spanner in the works aboard the *Mary Sue* but refrained from doing so. Morton did not seem to know about her, and for some reason Lazarus felt keen to keep it that way. She would no doubt attempt to kill Vasquez again and then he would make sure to find out who she was and settle the score.

"Yes..." he said, as he slid the Colt Starblazer into his empty holster and tucked the Belgian snub into his boot. "I have a feeling I'm going to have to recruit some help."

Chapter Three

The 3:10 from Yuma

The vast stretch of iron rails that cut through the burning landscape twinkled up at Lazarus in the morning sun. The land was silent, save for a light wind that rolled across the plains. From his position high up on the cliffs, he viewed the arid panorama with distaste. The railroad led to the State of Deseret, formally known as Utah, and the speeding hunk of steel and steam that thundered along its glistening path carried Gerard Vasquez to his appointment with the hangman.

Lazarus's horse nickered softly, and he rested his hand on the butt of the Colt Starblazer, aware of the dark patch of shadow that darted quickly behind a rock, ghostlike in the shimmering heat. It could have been a bird, but Lazarus knew better.

He had been aware that he was being shadowed ever since he had crawled out of the Colorado River, freezing, hatless and extremely grumpy. The shadow had followed him down the dusty streets of Yuma, hovering outside saloons whenever he took a drink. It was outside the shop when he had bought his new bowler hat. Lazarus wondered if the shadow had been loitering outside his hotel at night, looking up at his window while he had been sleeping. It was an unpleasant thought.

Wherever Lazarus had gone, *he* had been watching and following, his dark features concealed by a wide-brimmed hat and a long poncho concealing much more than just a powerful frame. In Yuma there had been no opportunity for him to make his move on Lazarus, but out here in the desert, where not another soul's shadow fell for miles around, it was very different.

A light footstep—no more than a whisper—fell behind Lazarus. He whirled around, drawing and cocking his revolver with lightning speed. For a while they stood staring at each other.

"If you're going to kill me, then you're wasting a good ally," Lazarus said.

Hok'ee glared at him from beneath the rim of his hat. His hair was long and jet, not greasy and matted like a white man's would be at that length, but sleek and shining. Enormous muscles rippled under his coppery skin, and he wore enough ammunition to fend off an army. Whatever his plan, it extended to more than merely killing him, and that pleased Lazarus.

"We're after the same chap, friend," said Lazarus, holstering his Starblazer. Whatever was concealed under that poncho was more than a match for a revolver, anyway. "How about we throw in our lot together and go at it as a deuce?"

The giant Navajo continued boring his hateful eyes into him. He evidently spoke no English or chose not to. Lazarus wondered if Vasquez communicated with his first mate in Navajo.

"Look, there's plenty of people aboard that train for us both to shoot," Lazarus continued. "I just want to get Vasquez off alive. I'm not a bounty hunter. I'm with the British government."

Hok'ee's eyes softened a little and he appeared to relax, although not showing complete trust.

"Vasquez will be in the second carriage," said Lazarus. "If we can get onboard, I think we should be able to pop in and surprise them without getting killed in the process. But we have to be quick. I take it you brought your own horse."

Hok'ee spat on the ground and beckoned Lazarus to follow. A fine mustang stood patiently further down the hill. They mounted up and descended the cliffs.

The train thundered through the landscape, belching steam like a mythical dragon. Lazarus and his new comrade galloped down the incline, hooves kicking up clouds of dust that would surely be visible from the train.

"It's too fast for us to match its speed for long, so we'll have to cross the tracks and fall back to the carriages," Lazarus shouted over the drumming hooves. "Our horses won't be able to keep up with us so we'll have to uncouple the carriages or disable the locomotive somehow. The driver will only be a mechanical," he suddenly realized what he had said and hurriedly added, "Oh, I beg your pardon, I didn't mean..."

Hok'ee snorted. "I'll cross first and draw their fire, sound good?"

Lazarus nearly fell of his horse in surprise. "You speak English!"

"You think all Navajo are dumb?"

"Well, no but... you're just a bit quiet, that's all."

"Why should I speak a language that is sour to my tongue? English is the language of those who have oppressed my people for generations. I use it sparingly."

Lazarus nodded sagely. "White man has not been good to your people."

Hok'ee grinned. "But white man gave me this to fight him with," and he whipped one side of his poncho away to reveal his right arm.

Lazarus gaped at the mass of bronze gears and iron plating that had been grafted on to his elbow. Like the Mecha-guard aboard the *Mary Sue*, it tapered into the muzzle of a Golgotha rifle with an automatic ammunition hopper. Too heavy for an average-sized man to carry, it took Hok'ee's massive strength to carry such a weapon, and on one arm at that. He broke away from Lazarus and crossed the tracks.

The train was coming up fast on their heels, and Lazarus could hear gunshots as Hok'ee made himself a target for the bounty hunters on board. With a deafening roar of air and chugging pistons, the locomotive passed. Lazarus caught glimpses of surprised faces in the first carriage, peering and pointing at him from the windows. He urged his horse closer and let the first two carriages drift by, making ready to duck should any of the bounty hunters take a shot at him.

No shots were fired. Hok'ee must have been making enough of a spectacle of himself on the other side of the tracks for them to pay much notice to Lazarus. The end of the third carriage appeared and Lazarus made ready to jump.

He seized the metal bar and swung his left leg over his saddle before leaping, seeing his horse vanish in the dust behind them. His foot nearly slipped on the runner, but he managed to get a firm grip and swung himself over the bar into the carriage.

He drew his Starblazer and flung open the door.

Rows of startled faces met him, but nobody stood to challenge him. He made his way along the swaying carriage to the door at the end. Passing from one to the other, he entered the second carriage and ducked just in time to dodge a bullet that splintered the woodwork by his left ear.

Taking cover behind some seats, he edged around to get a view of the carriage. Somebody stood up and fired again, but Lazarus was more concerned by the fact that they were wearing a dress. It was the woman from the *Mary Sue*.

"Well I'll be goddamned!" cried out Vasquez from somewhere. "I sure am popular these days. You're the fella that saved my life aboard the *Mary Sue*, ain'tcha?"

"Damned fool!" shouted the woman in that Eastern European accent of hers.

Lazarus was stumped. There appeared to be just the three of them in the carriage. He stood up slowly, holding his gun away from him in the universal signal for truce, but gripping it tight enough should he suddenly need it. "I don't know what the devil is going on here, but I've no interest in killing either of you."

"Bloody idiot..." began the woman.

"Holster it, lady," said Vasquez. "He ain't one of them. Come forward, partner, but if you try anything, we've enough firepower between us to give this carriage a nice new red coat. Now what say you tell us what you're about?"

"My name is Longman."

"You're a limey, ain't you?"

"I am in the service of Her Majesty, yes. I am here to escort you to the Confederate government on a matter of utmost importance."

At this Vasquez broke out into guffaws of laughter.

"I sure am the main attraction, ain't I?" he hooted, slapping his grimy britches and holstering his gun. "Here I was in manacles on my way to Great Salt Lake City for a pow-wow with President Blake, when this fine young thing bursts in here to seduce my guards right where I can see it all. Just when I thought my luck couldn't get any worse, somebody starts shooting at the train and all but one of them get up and high-tail it out of the carriage, leaving their comrade to guard me and have this fine lady all to himself. Lucky fella, I thought, until she shot him, of course." He indicated a body shoved behind a seat. Blood pooled under it. "I thought my number was up but then she cut me loose and gave me back my gun. Now you're here."

Lazarus glared at the woman. "What's your story? First you take a shot at him on the *Mary Sue* and now you're handing him his gun back?"

"There was a change in my orders," she replied, her tone curt.

"Orders from whom?"

"You work for your government and I work for mine."

"Which is?"

"That of His Majesty Tsar Alexander, the third of that name."

"She's a goddamn Russkie, friend," added Vasquez with a grin.

"I should have guessed as much," said Lazarus. Are you Okhrana?" The Okhrana were the Tsar's secret police, tasked with hunting down revolutionaries and anybody else who displeased the powers of Saint Petersburg. This did not limit them to Russia's borders. "What is Russia's interest in Vasquez?"

There was the sound of gunfire further down the

train.

"Do you want to discuss our foreign policy, Mr. Longman, or do you want to get off this train alive?"

Vasquez hooted. "I like this one! Now if my ears don't deceive me, that was a Golgotha rifle. Too heavy for ordinary men to carry. Is my pal Hok'ee aboard?"

"He got aboard some time ago," said the Russian. "But his horse was shot in the process. I saw it from the window. He managed to get aboard the last carriage."

Vasquez gave a low whistle. "He'll be mighty sore at that. He loved that horse."

"Well that throws a spanner in the works," said Lazarus. One horse between three... have you brought your own, Miss?"

"No."

"How did you get onboard? And how were you planning to get Vasquez off?"

"I was already onboard as a passenger before the train left Yuma. And I read the cargo inventory, which apparently you did not. The second to last car is loaded with horses."

"So your plan was to leap from a speeding train on horseback?"

"We'll have to uncouple the carriage and let it slow down, but yes, that was the essence of it."

"Sounds like a good enough plan to me," said Vasquez, drawing his revolver. "But we ain't gonna see it through if we stand around here jawing. Hok'ee is coming this way—I can hear his rifle talking—so the bounty hunters will be trapped between us."

"Agreed," said Lazarus.

"I didn't intend on carrying any extra weight off this train..." began the woman.

Lazarus smiled. "And I didn't intend on being carried, Miss...?"

"Katarina," she replied and pushed past him, flinging open the door.

The passengers were still in a state of terror in the next carriage, and the one following that. The fifth carriage was crowded, as if all the passengers from the next one had been herded in into it.

"Are you the law?" asked an elderly woman in a wide hat.

"No, Ma'am," replied Lazarus. "We're better than that."

The sound of shots could be heard from the next carriage. They went out onto the gangway. Vasquez crossed to the next carriage, opened the door a crack and peeped in.

"Three of them," he reported back.

"One each," replied Lazarus.

"Don't be so confident," Katarina replied. "How are we to get in there and take cover before they shoot us?"

"We go over their heads," said Vasquez.

"I don't believe this," said Katarina.

Vasquez clambered up onto the roof first and Lazarus—always the gentleman—stood aside to let Katarina go next. She shook her head at him.

"And have you gawking at my rear? I don't think so. You first."

Lazarus shrugged, and with an entirely involuntary image in his head of what her rear might look like through the folds of that dress, he clambered up after Vasquez.

The metal roof was scalding hot and Lazarus scrambled onto his knees and elbows as soon as he could to avoid any skin coming into contact with it. Ahead, Vasquez was on his feet, swaying back and forth in rhythm with the movement of the train. They made their way to the other end and dropped down onto the gangway to find themselves in the sights of a smoking Golgotha rifle.

"Hok'ee, old buddy!" said Vasquez. "This takes us back, eh? It's been a while since we've robbed a train."

"Well I hope your expertise in the area can get us off this one alive," Lazarus said, eying the door to the carriage with the gunmen inside. Its surface was peppered with bullet holes shot through from the other side.

"Piece of cake," replied Vasquez. "The next carriage looks like the horse car." He poked his head out and looked down the length of the train. "Yep. Last carriage before the post office car. This is where we get off, folks. Alright, start uncoupling the carriage, limey. Katarina, you and I will provide cover if any of those boys gets wise. Hok'ee, you know what to do with the door."

As the other three clambered onto the gangway of the horse car, Lazarus bent down and inspected the coupling mechanism. It was simple enough, and he soon had the last two carriages drifting away from the rest of the train. Hok'ee blasted through the lock to the horse car with his Golgotha and they filed into the dim, sweltering interior.

Just as Lazarus was about to enter, a bullet ricocheted off the iron banister an inch from him. He hit the deck as two more crunched into the wood. The bounty hunters were firing at him from the doorway of what was now the last carriage in the train and were a rapidly decreasing target. Lazarus thrust his hand into his right boot and pulled out the Belgian snub, cocked it, aimed and sent a slug towards the open door.

It struck the varnished wood and exploded, sending chunks of debris tearing into the gunmen. Smoke billowed from the open doorway, and the screams of wounded men could be heard briefly before the wind carried them away.

"Holy shit, friend!" Vasquez cried. "What does that limey government issue you with?"

"Belgian?" Katarina asked out of professional interest.

Lazarus nodded. "Fresh off the line."

Lazarus had noticed that Katarina's own pistol was a Smith and Wesson Model 3 Russian with an unusually long barrel. It appeared to be silver plated and was an exquisite piece, engraved with swirling Art Nouveau motifs. She raised the hem of her skirt to reveal the pale skin of her long, slender right thigh. Lazarus and Vasquez goggled at it but she didn't seem to care. Strapped to the flesh was a holster, into which she slid her revolver before sweeping her dress back into place. She caught them looking at her.

"I don't know why women always carry those silly little snub pistols in their handbags when there is plenty of room for something much more powerful under our skirts," she said.

"Um, quite," said Lazarus, knowing that he was flushed from something other than the stifling heat.

They made their way into the horse car and pushed past the sweating flanks of the beasts towards the door. Hok'ee had already picked out the four best horses for them.

"Alright, crew, this is our stop coming up!" Vasquez said, mounting his horse. The ceiling was low and he had to lean forward over the animal's neck. Katarina did the same, her attractively curled hair just brushing the ceiling. "Hok'ee, open her up!"

The Navajo slid the wide side door open. The dust whirled into the carriage, making the horses nicker and stamp their feet nervously. Lazarus shielded his eyes.

"Are you sure about this?" he shouted.

"Know any better way off a train, Englishman?" Katarina cried back.

"We could wait until the carriage comes to a standstill!" he suggested.

"And risk the authorities or more of that bounty hunting gang catching up with us?"

"Quit jawing, you lily-livered cowards and follow me!" cried Vasquez. "If both of you want me then you'll have to catch me!" and with a chuckle he spurred his horse into a leap that took him out into the sunlight and down and away, galloping hard and fast into the dust. Hok'ee followed, leaving Lazarus and Katarina gaping at the feat they had just witnessed.

"Does it occur to you that they may be making a run for it?" Lazarus mused aloud.

Katarina did not answer but instead leapt forward, her shapely figure astride her mount vanishing into the dust. Lazarus took a deep breath as if he were about to perform a high-dive and took the plunge.

Chapter Four

In which our hero is afforded a bird's eye view of Arizona Territory

The sun set across the vast flats of Arizona, stretching the shadows of the plateaus long and thin. The blistering heat of the day quickly evaporated as darkness filled the deep valleys. All the cold-blooded creatures that had been sunning themselves on the rocks vanished into their holes to escape freezing.

Lazarus's face was a mask of sweat and dust. They had been riding for a long time, and both horses and riders were tiring. Vasquez led the way with Hok'ee at his side and the other two trailing behind, unused to such lengthy periods of harsh travel. Katarina, in her thin bodice, was visibly cold however hard she was trying to hide it. Lazarus took off his jacket and held it out to her. She studied him hard before taking it.

"This doesn't mean we are friends, Englishman."

"Can you not call me Longman? Or Lazarus, perhaps."

"Lazarus? What a name!" she said, taking his coat.

"I just don't want to see you freeze to death before we get to our destination."

"Wherever that is," Katarina replied, looking ahead at Vasquez.

Owing to their having no water and empty

stomachs, Vasquez had offered to take them both to his temporary lair that lay less than a night's ride away. Considering that they were both trying to abduct him—and in Katarina's case, had even tried to kill him once—this was considered a mightily generous gesture by all concerned.

"What does the Tsar want with Vasquez anyway?" Lazarus asked Katarina, pleased to see that she had warmed up a little under his jacket that was two sizes too big for her.

"Nosy. What does Queen Victoria want with him?"

"Well, I don't suppose Her Majesty knows anything about him. But the people within her government that I work for are greatly concerned that he is kept alive and delivered into Confederate hands."

"My task is much the same."

"And yet you tried to kill him only a few nights ago."

"That was my original brief, yes. But after his true value was brought to our attention, I was given new orders to protect and escort him."

"As we both appear to be pursuing the same end, wouldn't you say that Britain and Russia could be allies in this affair?" Lazarus suggested. "No need to threaten each other or stand in each other's way."

Katarina smiled. "A lovely thought, Longman. There is just one problem."

"Oh?"

"I am escorting Vasquez to the Unionist partisans, not the Confederate government."

Lazarus groaned aloud. He should have known. Relations between Russia and Britain had been poor ever since that debacle in the Crimea. With the Civil War that had raged across the American continent and the ensuing stalemate, it only made sense that they would both support opposing sides. The British Empire needed its trade links with the southern states, and Tsar Alexander had been friendly to the Union since the beginning.

Vasquez, who had been listening to this conversation, hooted with laughter and fell back to join them. "Well, what a pretty pickle this is! Two foreign agents want to be my best friend and I get to sell my services to the highest bidder!"

"Now, Vasquez," said Lazarus, "there has never been any talk of purchasing your services. My orders are to escort you, by force if necessary."

"As are mine," said Katarina. "And to dispose of anybody who gets in the way, got that Longman?"

Lazarus sighed. Vasquez was right. It was a pretty pickle indeed.

They were high above the desert now, amid the peaks and plateaus of the mountain passes. The ground leveled out into the likeness of a gigantic billiard table. The stars were out, and with no cloud cover Lazarus felt the heat rushing out of his body, leaving him with a feeling of nakedness.

When they had reached the center of a plateau, Vasquez and Hok'ee dismounted. Lazarus and Katarina looked around. The plateau was devoid of anything that Lazarus could see might be of interest.

The two bandits crossed the flat area of rock to where a clump of dry bushes grew. With several mighty heaves, they pulled back the foliage—which wasn't as securely attached to the ground as Lazarus had assumed—and cast it aside. The ground beneath them seemed soft, like a skin on cream. Vasquez and Hok'ee began tugging at it on one side and it came loose, unfurling and billowing up clouds of dust, and Lazarus realized that it was a simple sheet of canvas.

They walked forward and found themselves standing on the edge of a large basin that had been hollowed out of the rock and concealed by the canvas. In the bottom of the crater was a vessel the size of a small fishing steamer. Its little brass portholes and single funnel made it appear ludicrously out of place in the rocky passes of the Southwest.

They climbed down into the crater. Lazarus recognized the vessel as a small military dirigible of the interceptor class. A logo of a corseted dance hall girl had been painted on its side, sitting astride a bomb with the words, 'Terror from Above!' banded around her. As Lazarus inspected it, he saw that it had been painted over what looked like the symbol for the Confederate Dirigible Corps.

"Ladies and gentlemen!" announced Vasquez, with one foot on the ladder, 'meet the *Santa Bella*!"

The interior of the vessel was as unmilitary as anything Lazarus might have expected. A covered cockpit showed the brass knobs, levers and dials involved in piloting the airship, but they were poorly polished. Above the varnished wooden steering wheel was a calendar showing various ladies painted by an artist who apparently hadn't mastered female clothing and had decided to do away with such frivolities entirely.

The cabin had a table and cushioned bench seating, and beyond there was evidence of two unmade beds. There was a little pot-bellied stove covered in a layer of grease and grime, and many unwashed pots and pans lay cluttered about.

"Home sweet home," said Vasquez cheerfully,

tossing his hat into a corner. "Hok'ee's getting a head of steam up so we'll soon be out of here."

"Wait a minute!" said Katarina, following Vasquez back out on deck. "Where are we going? I'm the one taking you into custody, not the other way around."

"Not on my ship, lady! Here you do as I tell ya!"

"But what's your plan, Vasquez?" Lazarus asked.

Vasquez grinned at him as he jammed a cheroot into his mouth and lit it with a match. "I know why you're both on my tail, even if you won't tell each other. Your respective governments are after that map of ours. Am I right?"

Lazarus eyed Katarina and saw that she was doing the same to him.

"Well, I'm done with the Confederate army," Vasquez continued, "and I have no real desire to throw in my lot with the Yankees, so I was thinking the best plan was to fetch the damned thing and hold ourselves a little auction. Whoever pays me the most gets it and can take it to their chosen camp without my having to come with! Now don't worry, we'll hold the auction on safe ground and I'll give you both plenty of time to wire your respective governments for money. I'm not sure how things'll pan out after that. One of you is likely to shoot the other, but once I'm sailing away with my money, it won't be my problem!"

Lazarus and Katarina stared at each other as their host went about the business of preparing the vessel for its journey. They were clearly thinking the same thing. This whole affair had got wildly out of hand and the future for one of them looked bleak. *But which one?*

"Either of you two gawking Gladys's ever been onboard a dirigible before?" Vasquez called over to them as he wrestled with one in a series of six trapdoors set into the vessel's deck.

They both shook their heads. Lazarus had heard of the devastating effects these craft had wreaked on the unprepared Union troops. It was the Confederate Dirigible Corps that had bombed New York City and Boston into smoking ruins.

"They're a vast improvement on the old design," commented Vasquez. "The early ones had a rigid shell and could only travel at five miles per hour. This craft has limp balloons and so is much lighter." He jerked a lever in the cockpit and there was a loud hissing sound. Balloons began to inflate from the six trapdoors.

"Isn't hydrogen flammable?" Lazarus asked, looking nervously at the smoking cheroot that hung from Vasquez's mouth.

"Sure is. None aboard this baby, though. Helium, folks. It's the new thing. Discovered by some eggheads in France. All airships use it now."

They stood and watched in awe as the light material began to rise higher and higher, expanding and billowing outwards, lifting the craft clean off the ground. Gas filled all the creases and soon the entire deck was shadowed by a monolithic balloon cluster. The anchor ropes strained and creaked as the craft bobbed in midair.

They went below deck. Hok'ee was in the furnace room, bathed in purple light as he shoveled mechanite into the glowing maw.

"How's she doing?" Vasquez hollered.

Hok'ee replied in Navajo and Lazarus realized for the first time that Vasquez must have a good understanding of the language, considering his first mate's reluctance to use English. They waited for the steam pressure to build up and then, by pulling a series of brass levers and knobs, Vasquez put into motion the great rear propellers that drove the craft forward. They drew in the anchor lines and soon they were drifting high and sailing north east through the starry clouds with the chasms and plateaus of the desert far below them.

By the lights of the gas lamps they sat in the cabin with the door shut against the chill air and inhaled the smell of cooking bacon and eggs and canned beans as Vasquez prepared their meal. The smells reminded Lazarus of his favorite greasy spoon in London's East End and, overcome by a sudden and unexpected pang of homesickness, he promised himself a meal there as soon as he got back. But for now, Vasquez's culinary efforts would have to do.

"Soup's on!" said Vasquez, sliding three plates across the lacquered tabletop. Hok'ee entered and sat down, seizing his fork and digging in. Katarina poked around at her plate with evident distaste. Vasquez sat down and began dousing Tabasco sauce over his plate with liberal carelessness. They watched him shovel the food down in great forkfuls.

"So where is it we are headed, exactly?" Lazarus asked Vasquez.

"You'll find that out when we get there," the bandit replied with a grin.

"There's really no call to be so cagey."

"Oh, there ain't? Well how come you two can't even bring up the matter of what we're all chasing after, then? It's Cibola, isn't it?"

Lazarus and Katarina looked at each other.

"And you claim to know its location," said Lazarus.

"All I claim is to know the location of the map. That's what you want, isn't it?"

"What good is a map to a place that doesn't exist?" said Lazarus.

"You don't sound very convinced that the matter is genuine," said Katarina.

"I'm not."

Vasquez dropped his fork with a clatter. "Now listen, limey, you're the one on my tail, hounding me for the map. Now all of a sudden you don't believe I've got the goods?"

"Oh, I believe you've seen a map. Maybe even have it hidden away somewhere. I just don't believe the seven golden cities of Cibola exist outside of fairy tales told to the Spaniards by the natives."

"Get a load of this guy, Hok'ee!" Vasquez crowed.

The Navajo was watching Lazarus intently with his sullen, black eyes. The Golgotha rifle had been detached from his elbow, and in place of it he had screwed on a hook that served as a multi-purpose tool for tinkering about on the ship. He rapped this on the tabletop slowly.

"He aims to tell us how things are running in this here country of ours. What makes you such a goddamned expert?"

"He's a historian," said Katarina. "And a grave robber."

"Archaeologist," Lazarus corrected, surprised that she knew so much about him. No doubt a file on him had been provided by the Russian government.

"Egghead, huh?" said Vasquez. "So, you know all about Cibola. More than me, perhaps?"

Lazarus sighed and began the tale from the beginning. "I know that in fifteen-thirty-six four survivors from a Spanish shipwreck resurfaced in Mexico. With them was a Moorish slave called

Estevanico; the first African to set foot in America. They had been wandering for eight years throughout the Southwest and had heard tales of a wealthy land to the north. The Spaniards in Mexico, who had recently amassed vast wealth from plundering the Aztec and Inca empires, became convinced that there must be a third golden empire in the northern continent. The Spanish had their own legend of seven bishops who fled Spain with all their wealth during the Moorish invasion hundreds of years previously. They believed that these bishops had set up seven golden cities in an unchartered land to the west. With the stories told by Estevanico and his companions, it seemed possible that these cities were somewhere in the American Southwest.

"The Viceroy of New Spain sent out an expedition under a Franciscan monk called Marcos de Niza who, with Estevanico as his guide, headed north to find this golden empire. Estevanico was an impetuous fellow by all accounts, who kept running on ahead and sending back promising clues. It seemed that they were drawing near to their goal. In one letter he said that he had found a fabulous city called Cibola, the first of many of its kind. Then, Estevanico drops off the map."

"De Niza tried to catch up with him," said Katarina, demonstrating that she too had been filled in on the fairy tale. "But he came across several members of Estevanico's party who were bloodied and beaten. They told him that the Moor had been killed at Cibola."

"Correct," said Lazarus. "De Niza dared not enter the city and only saw it from a distance. When he returned to Mexico City, he told what he had seen but mentioned nothing of gold. This did not perturb the

Spaniards, who were more convinced than ever that this Cibola and its sister cities must be the golden empire they sought. Another expedition was organized with de Niza as a guide and the governor of Nueva Galicia—a man called Coronado—as its leader.

"Coronado," put in Vasquez. "Now there's a fella I heard tell of."

"And with good reason," said Lazarus. "Not just because you share his name. Francisco Vazquez de Coronado was the fellow who exposed the whole thing as a fraud, however inadvertently. When he and de Niza arrived at Cibola, they found only a meager Zuni pueblo called Hawikuh. With Coronado and his men cursing de Niza as a phony, a battle broke out with the Zuni warriors, and the pueblo fell to the Spaniards."

"So, Coronado and his pals hadn't found Cibola, then?" asked Vasquez.

"That's a matter of opinion," said Lazarus. "There is no doubt that they found the city Estevanico had dubbed Cibola, but nobody had ever said anything about it being a city of gold. That was just in the imaginations of the Spaniards. And it was a myth the Zuni and other pueblo peoples were happy to propagate. Soon Coronado was heading out again on instructions given to him by the defeated Zuni, that golden cities lay further north east. He got as far as Kansas before giving up and returning in debt and in disgrace."

"So he didn't find it," said Vasquez, lighting up another cheroot. "That don't mean it don't exist."

"Its existence is highly unlikely," said Lazarus. "This continent has been occupied by white men for over four hundred years. Seven cities made of gold couldn't have escaped notice for that long."

"As you said, opinions are opinions," said Vasquez. "All I'm saying is I've got a map which is yours for the right price."

"My mission was to deliver you, not a map," said Lazarus.

"Well no dice on that one. It's the map or a mouthful of dust. You'll have to make your mind up on that."

Chapter Five

In which a mountain journey ends in betrayal

They spent the following morning drifting towards the mountains which hove into sight like golden teeth. By noon, Vasquez and Hok'ee were making plans to set the balloon down. Lazarus squinted into the distance, shielding his eyes against the glare. At the foot of the mountains he could see the ruins of what looked like an old fort. The wooden palisade had collapsed in places and there seemed to be no life about at all.

"What's this place?" Lazarus asked.

"An old outpost from the early days of the war," Vasquez replied. "It was once the northernmost airship dock in Arizona Territory, but it's fallen into disrepair now. We use it occasionally as a hideaway. Most of its various functions still work, and I keep a few supplies stockpiled."

They drifted over the base and Vasquez began to inflate the ballonets; balloons within the balloons that were slowly filled with air, compressing the helium which caused the dirigible to slowly sink. When they were a few feet from the dock, Hok'ee leapt overboard to secure the anchor lines.

Lazarus was glad to feel solid ground beneath his feet and looked around the abandoned base with interest. The buildings were in a poor state of repair—

broken windows and dusty timbers with tangles of dry desert growth in every crack. The rusty carriages for anti-airship batteries were visible beneath the overgrowth, their guns long since towed away. There was a dilapidated telegraph shack, but Lazarus could see no telegraph wires leading away from the fort and assumed that the Confederacy must have used a ground wire.

"I got weapons stored in a bunker under the main building," Vasquez said. "We're running low on helium, too. There's a store of that over there," he said, pointing at a storage building that had once supplied the airship docks. "This is as far as the *Santa Bella* goes, but I want her fitted out for a quick extraction once we're done."

"We're going on by foot?" Lazarus asked.

"I ain't risking her up in the mountains where there's no flat ground to land on. Hok'ee and I'll fetch the helium. You two head over to the main building and make yourselves comfortable. We'll fetch the supplies and eat before setting out."

Lazarus and Katarina found the main building swept, tidy and surprisingly well stocked considering the dilapidated state of the base.

"I wonder if any other bandits use this place," said Katarina. "It seems too neat to be the sole responsibility of those two."

"Well, there are plenty of rogues in these parts," Lazarus replied as he kindled the stove. "Although Vasquez is the only one I've heard of with his own airship. Civilian airships are forbidden. Airspace is for military craft only."

"I can't imagine that man in any sort of military outfit," she said.

"Well, he didn't last long. They gave him the boot years ago."

"Do you know why?"

"No. But it cost them one of their dirigibles."

Katarina was poking about in cupboards and opening doors to other rooms filled with junk and dust. "I wonder where he keeps his weapons."

"He said there was a bunker under the main building."

"I don't see any trap door," she replied, tracing lines in the dirt with the toe of her boot. "Maybe the entrance is outside."

"Why don't we wait until Vasquez and Hok'ee get back? I don't see why we need more weapons, anyway. You and I are both armed adequately."

"We're going into the mountains. In Russia, one never goes into the mountains without a good rifle. Too many wolves. And here there are mountain lions, bobcats and other things. Besides, do you trust Vasquez?"

"Trust him? Not nearly as far as I might throw him."

"My thoughts exactly. I want to see what else he's hiding. Stay here if you want, Englishman."

Lazarus sighed and drew an armchair towards the fire as she went out. She was lovely to look at, there was no getting around that. But she was as prickly as an Arizona cactus, and if he trusted Vasquez little, he trusted her less.

She was back before Vasquez and Hok'ee had returned. "Find anything?" he asked her.

"There's a trapdoor out back but it's padlocked."

"I wouldn't have thought a padlock would stop a woman like you."

"And what do you mean by that?"

"Only that your dress and corset seem to be the only things that set you apart from the other killers and soldiers of fortune in this world."

She seemed offended by that. "I see. You Englishmen like your women in your cozy parlors pouring your tea and keeping your beds warm at night. Anything else frightens you, am I right. Tell me, Longman. Are you married?"

"Married? No, I think that steamer departed long ago for me."

"Why do you say that? You can't be any more than thirty. Or was there a special someone? Someone who couldn't—*or wouldn't*—marry you and now you insist on playing the broken-hearted man of a tragic novel?"

Lazarus narrowed his eyes at her. "Has anybody ever accused you of being too forward? Or are all Russians like that?"

She sniffed. "You only despise my forwardness because you secretly wish you could be so yourself. But you're just too English. Your repressed nature simply won't let you."

Lazarus felt a decidedly uncharacteristic flare of patriotism. "If all Englishmen were as reserved as you seem to believe, then our Empire would surely never have cloaked half the globe."

She smiled. "Oh dear, have I offended your honor?"

He immediately felt foolish. How had this woman ignited a flame of pride in him for his homeland that he had thought long snuffed out? He had once been a proud Englishman, but a war in Africa and four years of doing the bureau's dirty work had sapped his store of patriotism.

Vasquez poked his head around the door. "Why don't I smell cooking?" he asked. "You two sure look comfortable while Hok'ee and I have been doing all the heavy lifting. There's tins in the cupboard and biscuits somewhere too."

Lazarus looked to Katarina. She frowned at him. "Are you honestly expecting me to cook for everybody just because I'm the one in the dress and corset?"

"Oh, for goodness sake!" said Lazarus, rising. "I'll get the tins, you find the biscuits. Playing happy families with you isn't exactly what I signed on for either."

When they were done, they made ready to set out. Vasquez produced a key for the bunker and began passing items out to Hok'ee. One was an enormous Jericho Gatling gun which Hok'ee attached to his mechanized elbow. Its six barrels were automatically cranked by some internal switch over which Hok'ee had control. It had its own miniature furnace and boiler which could be powered by a tiny flake of mechanite. The weight of the thing made Lazarus realize that the mechanical implants in his body must be grafted onto his skeleton and he wondered how much of the bone under the flesh had metal attached to it to make the weight seem insignificant. In addition, he was even able to toss a couple of bandolas of ammunition over his shoulder.

"What on earth is up in those mountains that warrants that kind of firepower?" Lazarus asked.

"You never know," Vasquez replied. "Bandits like myself; quite a few of whom hate my guts. Bounty hunters. And the Unionist Partisan Rebels pop up all over this territory. You can never be too careful."

They set off into the mountains with Hok'ee

guarding their backs and Vasquez leading the way. Great canyons dropped down into the river, and towering sandstones and limestones in varying shades of red and orange that looked to Lazarus like an English layer cake rose up on all sides.

It was swelteringly hot and there was no shade. Lazarus drank sparingly from the canteen he had filled at the airship base, for he did not know how long this excursion was going to take, nor what would happen once they reached their objective. Would Katarina try to steal the map from him and leave him to die of thirst and heat up here in the mountains? Or would she just shoot him in cold blood? He dreaded every possibility and did not see any favorable outcome of this situation. He would kill her if he had to, but his gut churned at the thought of more blood on his hands.

"Here we are," said Vasquez at last.

This came as a relief to Lazarus, for their leader had shown the occasional sign of confusion at some marker that had been washed away or a bit of land he didn't remember. He pointed to a small cave entrance high up in the cliff face.

"You hid it in a cave?" Katarina asked, as if in disbelief that he could have chosen so foolish a spot. "Are you so sure that it hasn't been discovered? Or washed out by rainwater? Or chewed up by a bobcat?"

"Have a little faith, darlin'" he replied. "Ain't no bobcat gonna eat my map, nor rainwater get to it."

It was a tough scramble. Twice Lazarus offered his hand to Katarina, only to receive a burning look of resentment in return. They clambered into the cool shade, and Lazarus could have wept at the relief. The cave was deep and fell away into chilled darkness. The ground was soft from the silt that the river had deposited in it untold centuries ago. Vasquez drew a gas lamp from his knapsack and got it going, illuminating the deep shadows and smooth rock formations.

They walked on slowly, inching forward only as far as the lamp would illuminate. Vasquez held his pistol out, cocked. "There might be a mountain lion and her cubs in here, so stay close and make ready with your firearms," he cautioned.

A passageway led off from the tunnel, and Lazarus realized that most of it must have been hollowed out by the hands of natives centuries ago.

"Stop," Vasquez commanded. He knelt down and began sweeping the dusty floor with one hand. "Pass me the shovel, Hok'ee."

The shovel was passed—a simple folding one instantly recognizable to the military man—and Vasquez began to dig, churning up dirt and loose rubble. He appeared to strike something that brought him immense pleasure, for he flung aside his shovel and began digging with his hands. He eventually removed a tin ammunition box from the ground—rusted, dented and scarred.

"Let's see it, then," said Lazarus.

Vasquez bundled it under his arm. "Not so keen, limey. Let's get out of this cave first and into daylight. Then I'll say what happens next."

They made their way out, and Lazarus was just assessing the best way down the cliff face when a shot rang out and flaked off a chunk of rock by his feet with a loud 'ping!'

They all hit the dirt, and Lazarus drew his Starblazer. He could see men moving about down in the valley, and his first thought was that they had walked into a trap planned by Vasquez. But then he saw their uniforms. They were blue. Long dusters with stars and stripes on the arms. Some wore hats with crossed sabers. *Yankees.*

"We got you surrounded, Vasquez!" somebody cried out.

Hok'ee flipped open the carousel magazine in his Jericho and fed in a band of ammunition.

"No!" said Lazarus. "There's too many!"

"Boy, you never seen Hok'ee and his Jericho in action!" said Vasquez. "He can wipe out a squad in ten seconds flat!"

"They have snipers concealed in the bushes," Lazarus insisted. "He'll be killed before he pulls the trigger."

Vasquez poked his head above cover, then ducked immediately as a bullet ricocheted near his ear. "Alright, Hok'ee. Cool it while we think this over."

"This is the Unionist Partisan Rangers!" called up the voice again. "Come down with your guns holstered!"

"Rebels! How the hell did they find us?" Vasquez demanded.

"Let's do as they say and see what they want," said Katarina. She stood up slowly and slid her long pistol back into its holster, concealing it with her dress. Lazarus watched her, half expecting her head to get blown off at any second. She raised her arms and called down, "We surrender!"

"Woman's not as tough as she puts on," Vasquez mumbled. "But she has a point. I don't see any other way out of this."

"Maybe we can bargain with them," Lazarus suggested.

"Maybe. But you keep your yap shut about what I've got in this here box. I didn't dig it up for these blue boys to get hold of."

They stood up together. After much encouragement, the reluctant Hok'ee joined them and they made their way down the cliff towards the partisans.

They were a rag-tag group. Uniform was only adhered to in the navy blue of their garments and a few Union insignias, for they wore a variety of dusters, cavalry trousers and tatty coats. Their leader, a tall, thin black man stepped forward. "My name is Lieutenant Clay Thompson of the Unionist Partisan Rangers," he said. "You are hereby under arrest in the name of the United States of America. Please hand over your firearms."

Lazarus and Vasquez reluctantly let the rebels seize their guns, although nobody thought to check their boots. Lazarus afforded himself an inward smile.

"Christ, how do we get this thing off?" one of the rebels exclaimed, pointing at Hok'ee's right arm.

"You prize it loose from my dead body," Hok'ee replied through a snarl.

"If you insist," said Lieutenant Thompson. "But I'd rather keep you all alive. For the time being."

After much coaxing from Vasquez and Lazarus, Hok'ee was finally convinced to unhinge the mighty Jericho gun. It took two men to lift it off his body and carry it away. The mini-furnace was still hot, and they also took his supply of mechanite. It was only then that Lazarus noticed that Katarina was still armed.

"Do they have the map, Miss Mikolavna?" Lieutenant Thompson asked her.

"It's in the box under his arm," she replied. "He just

dug it up."

The three of them gaped at her. Then Vasquez exploded. "Goddamned hussy! You're with the rebs? Why did I ever trust a Russian?"

She smiled at him. "You were always going to end up in Unionist hands, Vasquez. This way just happened to be the most efficient."

Lazarus felt sick. He had been a fool to trust her. And now that her mission was complete, he was more or less disposable in her eyes. Would they kill him now? It was odd that he felt more hurt by the fact that he had been tricked by her than by the possibility of his imminent death.

"How did you let them know where we were?" Vasquez asked her.

"Does that old telegraph shack back at the fort still work, by any chance?" Lazarus asked him.

"Sure does. I've used it myself a few times to call in supplies from friends."

"Then I imagine that these rebels have tapped into it. She radioed them on the sly. I let her out of my sight for all of ten minutes."

"Remarkably astute, Englishman," replied Lieutenant Thompson. "I can see that you are one to watch out for. Captain Townsend will decide what is to be done with you back at base. But it's getting late, so, if you don't mind, we'll move out now."

They followed the river downstream, with the towering canyon walls on either side shading them from the setting sun. It was much cooler now.

"No hard feelings, Longman?" Katarina said, sidling up to Lazarus. "We both had a job to do."

"But your job might get me executed as a foreign spy," he replied sourly.

"Don't be like that. Would it have been any different if you had had the upper hand? Why didn't you call in your own help?"

"Because I'm not a backstabbing so-and-so," he replied, unable to think of any biting insult that was suitable. "Besides, how long have you been in with these fellows? Did your Russian contacts set you up with them?"

"Actually, they sought me out. My mission was to kill Vasquez. But when Captain Townsend and Lieutenant Thompson here informed me that he was worth more to the partisans alive than dead, I wired Moscow and received new orders."

"To get Vasquez into the hands of the U.P.R."

"Precisely."

"So what's the plan? Ship him north to the Union?"

"I imagine so. Or keep him here. That's up to Captain Townsend. My job is done."

"And me? I suppose I'm done too."

She looked away when he said that. "I'll put in a good word for you when we get to their base. I can't promise anything, but I'll do my best to ensure that you are not..."

"Killed?"

"Exactly."

Chapter Six

In which the Rebel Underground is revealed

Darkness had fallen by the time they arrived at the abandoned mine. A great basin had been cut into the rock and several dilapidated huts stood around, surrounded by the rusting wreckage of machinery.

"Is this your base?" Lazarus asked Lieutenant Thompson.

"Just a back door," he replied.

They descended into the basin and, with cautious glances from their captors, began to file into the black mouth of a mining shaft.

"I ain't too crazy about going underground," said Vasquez. "How recently were these supports reinforced?"

"Shut it, Vasquez," replied one of the rebels.

Lazarus looked at the timber supports and had to admit that they seemed to be in very good condition, considering the age of the mine.

They wandered deeper and deeper underground, their way lit only by the flickering gas lamps the rebels carried. A second shaft crossed their way, and it was laid with rails. A large vehicle that looked to be some sort of transportation stood nearby, its furnace hot and ready. A rebel poked his head up from the cab and hailed Thompson.

"Ready to go?" Thompson called up to him.

"Like a horny bull in a pen!" came the answer.

"Load up the prisoners!"

They were manhandled up into the seating compartment of the locomotive, which was lined with benches. Rebels sat between them, their rifles planted stock down. The engineer opened the throttle and the wheels gradually began to turn, picking up speed. Soon they were hurtling down the track with nothing to see around them but darkness.

Lazarus had a hundred questions he wanted to ask about this underground railway that was similar to the one in London, only much more primitive. But the noise of the pistons and cylinders was deafening and made any attempts at talking pointless. It even felt like they changed lines at some point, indication that a huge underground network was in use by the rebels.

They travelled for what felt like several hours, eventually slowing down and emerging into a cavernous area lit by gas lamps. Lazarus was reminded of Charing Cross Station. There were two platforms and several sidings. Men and women in unionist attire loaded and unloaded carriages of supplies. There were one or two mechanicals doing the more heavy-duty work.

"You rebels sure have been busy bees," Vasquez remarked.

Lieutenant Thompson was evidently pleased and began telling them all about it. "Our movement was once called the 'Underground Railroad' at the beginning of the war. It was designed to help escaped slaves flee to the north. I was only twelve when my older brother and I ran away from our plantation in Louisiana. There was no physical railroad then of course, just kind farmers and abolitionists who organized the transportation and feeding of many such as us. We travelled at night, sleeping in barns during the day, until we reached the north and freedom.

"And yet you came back to the south," said Katarina.

He nodded firmly. "To help others such as myself."

"But there are no more slaves," Lazarus said. "Not since the Emancipation Act."

"But the Confederacy is still in effect. You call us rebels, well they are the real rebels—a thorn in the side of the United States. Now, with supplies of mechanite and the technology available, we can *really* have an underground railroad. Soon, we will join up with the Union and then there won't be a thing to stop us from totally undermining the C.S.A. Folks can come and go as they please."

"And you can pop up and harass the government before vanishing into your holes like rabbits," said Vasquez in a scoffing tone.

"The only government I recognize is that of the United States of America." He hailed a fellow lieutenant. "Where's the captain?"

"Down at the Worm," came the reply.

Lazarus wondered what exactly 'the Worm' was, but they were apparently about to find out. Lieutenant Thompson and his squad led them down a tunnel that diverged away from the main line. The sides of the tunnel were circular, as if gouged out by a scooping tool. Workers were laying rails on the ground. They took another locomotive and plunged into darkness yet again.

There was a rumbling noise ahead that grew gradually louder, eventually blocking out even the noise from the locomotive. In the darkness ahead, they could make out the shape of some iron behemoth, moving, shuffling away from them at a slow but steady pace. They clambered out and walked towards it. Steam and dust filled the air and the heat was fierce. The back portion of the machine was open and a mining cart on rollers rumbled out from its innards, loaded with rubble. Men in overalls pushed it along parallel rails until it was side by side with the locomotive that had brought them.

Thompson leapt up a small flight of steps in the rear of the monstrous construction and rapped on a riveted door. It swung open and a face smeared with dust, oil and sweat poked out. It threw up a quick salute.

"Tell the captain I have the prisoners," Thompson said.

"Yessir!"

Before long, a woman appeared and jumped down from the Worm. As well as her elfin face with its high cheekbones, Lazarus could only assume she was a woman because she had long hair, although it was twisted into strange coils that looked heavy, straining against the string that tied them back behind her head. He had seen similar hairstyles on Greek Kouroi statues and bewigged ancient Egyptians. All other characteristics marked her out as a man; the oily trousers, the officer's jacket with the stars and stripes insignia, and the grim expression of one used to commanding respect written on her soot-streaked face.

"Captain Townsend," said Thompson, snapping to attention. "We have Vasquez, Hok'ee and the map. Plus the British agent."

Captain Townsend wiped her hands on an oily cloth and tossed it to the man behind her. "You're sure you have the map? You've seen it?"

"It's in here," Thompson said, handing her the iron box. "I thought it best to leave the honor of opening it to you."

She took the box and glanced at each of them in turn. She focused on Katarina. "And this must be the agent of our Russian friends. At last we meet." Her voice was chilly, as if she did not fully trust her foreign ally.

"I am Katarina Mikalovna," said Katarina, equally cold. They immediately seemed to dislike each other. Katarina was everything Townsend was not, feminine, sophisticated and elegant. But Townsend was not unattractive in her own way, pretty but dirty, a true diamond in the rough.

"We are indebted to you, Miss Mikalovna," replied the captain. "You shall be adequately rewarded. Now," she drummed her fingers on the sides of the metal box. "Let's head up to my office and see what we have here."

"How goes the drilling, Captain?" Lazarus heard Thompson ask, once they were back at the station and walking towards the row of buildings fronted with grimy glass panes.

"The Worm keeps getting jammed. Too much schist and granite. We might have to back it up again and replace the drill if it's been blunted."

"That will take time."

Lazarus took out his pocket watch and checked the compass set in its lid, out of interest. It made him feel a little better to know at least what pole they were facing. The newly dug tunnel was heading in a north westerly direction.

Townsend's office was a well-equipped if crowded

one that overlooked the platforms. There was a good deal of engineering tools and blueprints pinned on boards. Lazarus wondered if this captain had anything to do with the actual construction of her wonderful tunneling machine. Having seen how she commanded her men he did not put anything past her. There was very little in the way of a personal touch about the office, apart from a single framed photograph of a handsome man in a business suit. He wondered if he was her lover, and then, if he was still alive.

Captain Townsend sat down in her chair and placed the metal box on the desk in front of her. There were no locks, but the hinges were well rusted and they watched her struggle with it awhile before it popped open. Inside was something bundled in oiled cloth. She removed it and held it up to the light of the hurricane lamp on her desk.

It was a helmet—a type used by the Spanish, centuries before. An antique certainly, but Lazarus thought Vasquez had managed to pull a cunning trick on Townsend and was about to congratulate him, when he saw the lines inscribed on the surface of the helmet. Townsend had spotted them too, and was running her finger along rivers, canyons and mountain ranges that had been painstakingly etched into the metal with a sharp object. The helmet *was* the map.

"Ingenious," said Captain Townsend. "I wonder who made it."

"Folks say Estevanico did," replied Vasquez.

"The Moor? I was under the impression that he was killed by Zunis."

"Maybe he was. Maybe he wasn't. Maybe he passed the map on before he died."

Townsend's eyes glittered as she gazed upon the

inscribed map and the single word, 'Cibola' that hung somewhere in the southern part of the Colorado Plateau. "Put these men in irons," she said. "I'll conduct interrogations later."

The cells carved by the rebels lived up to any description of the dungeons of the middle ages. Rough-hewn rock formed the walls, and a door of thick wood reinforced with iron sealed them in, a tiny grate in it their only view of the corridor.

"Well, I'll be damned for a fool," said Vasquez once they had been left alone. "I should have known that Russian hussy was planning to backstab me. But I'm a sucker for a pretty dress. You should have let me kill her aboard the *Mary Sue*, limey. Then the map would be yours and I'd be a free man."

"I'm beginning to agree with you," Lazarus said.

"Beginning to? You're a soft one."

"When I get out of here," said Hok'ee slowly, his rage causing him to speak English, "I'll make that *Kiiya' sizini* wish she had never set foot in this land."

Lazarus looked out into the corridor. It was deserted. He turned to his comrades. "When they come to take us away for interrogation, I'll try and get them to pick me first. Here," he delved into his right boot and brought out the Belgian pistol and handed it to Vasquez.

"What the hell?" the bandit exclaimed, feeling the weight of it. "I'd forgotten about your little peashooter! It weighs a ton!"

"It should be powerful enough for you to break out of this cell and come and meet me."

"And what will you be doing?"

"Retrieving that map," Lazarus replied firmly. "Wait ten minutes before pulling the trigger."

Hok'ee leaned forward. "How are we to escape? We are underground. This weapon of yours won't blast through rock."

"There's tunnels enough for us to vanish into. It may be a long trek, but the rebels have many surface exits. We just need to find one before they find us."

A key grated in the lock. Vasquez shoved the revolver down the back of his britches just as Lieutenant Thompson entered the cell.

"Couldn't keep away from us, Lieutenant?" Lazarus asked. "Or has your queen got you running errands like a shoe-shine boy?"

Thompson's eyes blazed and he looked about ready to hit him. "Take this wise-ass first," he said to the men at his back. "I'm gonna enjoy seeing him try his wit on the captain."

Lazarus was manhandled out of the cell and marched up to Townsend's office where she was waiting for him. The conquistador helmet was still in the box on the desk.

"Have a seat, Mr...?"

"Longman." He plonked himself down in the chair opposite her desk without invitation.

"Tell me Mr. Longman. What is an Englishman doing in America?"

"Just his job."

"Which is?"

Lazarus smiled. "You have my map. I'd like it back."

"*My* map," Townsend corrected. "When I was a little girl, my granddaddy used to tell me stories about Cibola and the Seven Golden Cities. Then of course, I got involved in the rebel militias, and life became too hectic for fairy tales. But when I discovered that Cibola really existed and that the Confederate usurpers were after it, I realized that the quest for the golden cities and the quest for freedom was one and the same thing. Arizona Territory is my territory, Mr. Longman. And I will do what I must to ensure its freedom."

"You sound an awful lot like a Confederate in the old days," Lazarus commented. "Harping on about a single state's independence and freedom. I wonder, does that U.S. flag on your shoulder mean as much to you as it does to Lieutenant Thompson here?" He felt the lieutenant shift uneasily behind him. "He's quite the dreamer. Sees the United States as the land of freedom, and I'd hazard a wager that he thinks the plan is to ship Vasquez and the map to his friends in Colorado, so the real Union can decide what is to be done with them."

"Cibola is in Arizona," said Townsend. "The map stays here. We have the equipment and the manpower to retrieve it without involving the other states. And I'm sure my lieutenant understands this. Am I right, Lieutenant?"

"Right... Captain," said Thompson. Lazarus could hear the uncertainty in his voice and he smiled, seeing a lever with which he might be able to move a mountain.

"And of course, once you have found Cibola, as loyal partisans to the United States you would immediately ship the gold north using your underground railroad," Lazarus went on. "How far do you intend the railroad to reach, by the way? Denver? Or into Kansas, perhaps?"

She eyed him coldly. "Denver is the plan. Besides, the gold must first be found before I decide what is to be done with it."

"Before *you* decide..." Lazarus mused aloud. "A rebel from Arizona. This territory was never part of the United States for long, was it? One has to wonder how deeply your loyalties to the U.S. run."

This seemed to awaken something in Lieutenant Thompson, and he spoke up. "Captain, the gold must be delivered to the United States. Else what are we fighting for?"

Townsend glared at him. "Let's leave the interrogations of our prisoners to me, is that alright, Lieutenant?"

"Looks like your captain is running her own little state here, Thompson," said Lazarus. "Soon, she'll be declaring herself governor. Well I'll tell you something, Thompson. This new railroad you fellows are so busy burrowing isn't going in the direction of Denver. It's hard to tell this deep underground, unless you take the time to look at a compass, which I did not long ago. This tunnel doesn't head North East, but North West. Deeper into the mountains. Your captain has known the direction in which Cibola lies for a while now. All she needed was the map leading her to the gold before she could set herself up as a queen of this territory."

Thompson's lips tightened. He still only half believed Lazarus, that much was clear, but his hand had casually rested on the butt of his pistol, whether consciously or not. "Captain, is this true?" he asked.

"Lieutenant, you are stepping out of line," said Captain Townsend. "Leave us. I'll have somebody else take Mr. Longman back to his cell."

"Captain, I need an answer," said Thompson. "Have you rerouted the railroad without my knowledge?"

Townsend's eyes flared and she stood up, planting

her fists down on the table.

"Leave, Lieutenant! That's an order!"

Thompson's palm still rested on the butt of the pistol. Lazarus had hoped that he would have drawn it before Vasquez fulfilled the next part of his plan. It wasn't perfect, but when the explosion from the cells below shook the room, Lazarus decided that it would have to do.

As Townsend and Thompson looked about in surprise at the dancing picture frames on the wall and wobbling light while the deafening roar rumbled below them, Lazarus was on his feet. He barreled into Thompson and snatched the revolver from his holster before Captain Townsend had a chance to draw hers. He aimed it at her forehead and marched across the office, grabbing her around the middle and holding the barrel to her temple. Thompson looked on in helpless dismay. Lazarus took his hand from Townsend's middle long enough to snatch up the helmet in its box from the desk and shove it into his armpit.

A second explosion roared down the corridor outside, and Lazarus knew that Vasquez and Hok'ee were on the loose. *God help anybody who got in their way.* With Captain Townsend still his hostage, Lazarus backed out of the office and made his way down the hall, where dust was trickling down from the support beams.

Out in the station, chaos reigned. Rifles cracked and partisans ran this way and that, seeking cover and looking for weapons. The Worm had been backed out of the tunnel, and now that Lazarus could see it in its entirety, he thought its name apt enough. It was well over a hundred feet long and comprised of several iron ridges connected by a canvas canopy. These ridges moved independently, powered by hydraulic pistons so the whole thing could shuffle back and forth very much like a worm or caterpillar. On its front end was a massive drill mechanism, designed to plough through the rock so that each successive ridge on the Worm's body could shift forward and support the extra feet of freshly dug tunnel.

Lazarus could see Vasquez and Hok'ee taking cover on the side nearest to them. Somebody noticed Lazarus and took a shot, missing by several feet.

"Stop you fools!" cried out Townsend.

When it became known that their captain was held hostage, there were cries of "hold your fire!" and "He's got the captain!"

Lazarus whistled to Vasquez and Hok'ee to join him and, keeping their backs away from any soldiers, they slowly edged towards the tunnel they had come from.

"There's no way out, Longman," said a Russian voice. Katarina and a squad of soldiers had marshaled themselves on the tracks and had their guns trained on them. Lazarus could see the silver glint of her long barrel.

They began to edge backwards into the tunnel. Katarina and the rebels followed, pace for pace.

"We can't walk backwards the whole way," said Vasquez.

Lazarus looked up. They were in the tunnel now and carved rock encased them on all sides. "No," he agreed. "We can't." In a sudden move, he hurled Townsend from him and helped her forward with a boot to the posterior. As she stumbled, and Katarina and the soldiers beyond struggled to find their marks, Lazarus called for the Belgian snub. Vasquez tossed it to him and he pointed it at the ceiling of the tunnel. He squeezed the trigger and the ceiling erupted in an explosion of dirt, rubble and dust. It came down in a cascade between the rebels and the escapees, shielding Lazarus and his companions from fire by a wall of debris. They took to their heels and pounded down the tunnel.

"I hope some of those boulders crushed that bitch," panted Vasquez as they ran.

"Katarina or Townsend?" Lazarus asked.

"Take your pick."

The passageway lights soon petered out and they found themselves running in pitch darkness.

"How are we to find the way out?" Vasquez asked.

"I'm hoping the exits have gas lamps," Lazarus replied. "Or perhaps we will be able to see daylight."

They ran on until they could run no more. The darkness was absolute, and it felt like being underwater and not knowing which way was up. Sweat and dust plastered to them, they walked on, occasionally stumbling over the rails.

Lazarus felt suddenly cold. The chill underground air made the sweat on his body feel icy. But there was also a breeze and he started in alarm.

"Wait! There must be an exit somewhere close!"

"What makes you say that?" asked Vasquez somewhere behind him.

"Don't you feel the breeze? That's desert air coming down a mineshaft. Feel the walls."

They spread out, and after much tripping and searching the rough rock, it was Hok'ee who found the passageway that cut upwards to the left. They followed it up and as it turned a corner, they were dazzled by a white rectangle of light up ahead.

"Thank God," said Vasquez. "I need to breathe

good air and feel the sky over me instead of a mile of rock."

They staggered out of the mineshaft onto the desert plains.

"They must have places like this all over Arizona Territory," said Vasquez. "I must have been in a couple myself, hiding from the law or bounty hunters and never knew how far down they went."

"Well, Vasquez," said Lazarus. "You've had a taste of Unionist hospitality. What say you we stop this daft runaround and head to Fort Flagstaff and speak with the true government?"

"Government my ass," said Vasquez. "They'll likely shoot me for desertion. And that's just the first thing they'll shoot me for."

"But we have the map to Cibola. That has to count for something. With your cooperation and my recommendation, they'll have to welcome you as an ally. What do you say? I'm not entirely sure where we are, but Fort Flagstaff is the northernmost Confederate outpost. It can't be more than a day's walk."

"But we have no food or water."

"If we find a town, of course we'll stop, but my guess is Fort Flagstaff is our closest hope in any direction."

He was not convinced.

"Whatever we decide, we'd best get moving," Lazarus urged. "The rebels will be on our heels and Katarina will not rest until she finds us."

"Why should she care? Isn't her assignment over?"

"I don't know how far her orders extend. Her mission may include ensuring that the map remains in Unionist hands until they find Cibola. If that's the case then she won't let rock, fire or water stop her from killing us and getting that map back."

Chapter Seven

In which a change of heart is had at five thousand feet

They wandered across the Colorado Plateau, through endless miles of sparse acacias and ponderosa pines that at least provided occasional shade. Lazarus knew that the forest vanished into desert well before it reached Fort Flagstaff and grew worried that they would not find any water. They passed the ruins of a pueblo, blackened by fire and half of it blown away, as if by dynamite.

"Wonder what happened here," Vasquez commented.

"Bombed," said Lazarus. "Bombed from the air like New York and Boston."

"This wasn't a military target," said Vasquez. "Why bomb pueblos?"

It made Lazarus intensely uneasy. They were entering a restricted area, although nobody knew why it was off limits.

Fortunately, they came within sight of a Hualapai village and approached cautiously. They let Hok'ee do the talking as he had some knowledge of their language, and although the Navajo and the people of the plateau had often been at odds in the past, the Hualapai were cautiously welcoming, although initially wary at the sight of his metal attachments. They conversed a great deal and Vasquez did his best to translate to Lazarus, possessing a smattering of tribal languages himself.

"They're asking if we're warriors from the sky," he said. "Don't know much what that means, but they seem mighty frightened. They say that fire and death comes from the sky in these parts and has taken many lives."

"That probably has something to do with the ruined pueblo we passed," Lazarus said.

"Apparently many Hualapai have been pushed from their lands and many more killed," said Vasquez.

Once it was determined that they were not enemies from the sky, the Hualapai gave them food and water before wishing them well on their journey.

The desert consumed them. Lazarus and Vasquez sweated profusely under their hats and Lazarus marveled at Hok'ee who walked ahead of them, nothing on his head but his shining black hair and not a bead of sweat on his forehead.

As they neared Fort Flagstaff, a dirigible hove into view. The Confederate flag was emblazoned on its side and armed troops could be seen on its deck. It descended and threw out rope ladders, which the soldiers used to alight. A man in a captain's frock approached. "This is a restricted area," he said through his curling whiskers. "What's your business here?"

"I am an agent of the British Empire," said Lazarus. "We have something for the eyes of whoever is in charge at Fort Flagstaff."

The captain looked them over, not liking what he saw one bit. He took them on board, either as prisoners or passengers—they weren't sure—and they took off, ploughing through the air in a southerly direction.

A great bulge appeared in the mist. Rising up out of the desert dust was the biggest airship Lazarus had ever seen. It had a deck the size of several British destroyers welded together and had not one balloon, but several, clustered like swollen hemorrhoids. On the side of the largest was the Confederate flag, and beneath it in white block letters was written; *Fort Flagstaff II*. Lazarus began to understand why the Hualapai lived in fear.

"What in the hell is that?" asked Vasquez, his eyes wide.

"This here is Fort Flagstaff on the move," the captain answered. "It's the Confederate navy's greatest achievement. With five of these we could level the Union and win the war for good and all."

They descended into the shadow of the colossal balloons and on the deck below, Lazarus could make out several other dirigibles in dry docks, their balloons deflated. There were Interceptors like the *Santa Bella* as well as other, larger craft. He realized then that this was more than just a dirigible. It was a dirigible *carrier*. They landed and clambered down onto the wooden deck. The captain sent somebody to fetch the general while he oversaw the securing of his vessel.

A large man whose uniform had a white collar with three gold stars with a wreath on it marched over to them, flanked by several soldiers. He had wide side whiskers only touched with grey. "Gerard Vasquez," the general exclaimed. "My lucky day."

Vasquez's eyes blazed. "Reynolds! So those crazy bastards put you in charge of this airborne asylum. If my hands weren't manacled, I'd choke the life out of you."

Hok'ee suddenly lurched forward in a furious burst of rage, and nearly reached the General before he was clubbed down by four soldiers. He cursed in Navajo and they continued beating him until he barely had his senses left.

"General," said Lazarus, stepping forward, alarmed by the vitriolic reaction of his companions. "My name is Lazarus Longman, agent of the British Empire. I believe you have been in contact with my associate, Morton."

"Yes sir, I have indeed. We were expecting you many days ago."

"There have been some unfortunate diversions from the original plan, but here they are and here is the map." He held the iron box out.

"Limey, if you give the map to this man, I'll shoot you myself," said Vasquez.

Lazarus hesitated and then handed it over.

General Reynolds opened the box and looked inside. He smiled. "Let's adjourn to my office," he said. "It's mighty chilly out here on deck. Captain, escort the prisoners to the brig."

"General, these men have come here of their own free will to aid you," said Lazarus.

"Your mission was to deliver them to me," said the general. "They are dangerous criminals; one a deserter and the other an escaped prisoner."

"I gave them my word that I would vouch for them, Sir."

"Then you're a fool, begging your pardon. These men will shoot you in the back first chance they get. Now get them out of here!"

"General, I must insist," said Lazarus, wilting under Vasquez's stare as he and Hok'ee were hauled away, under arrest for the second time in the same number of days. "These men have been the very word of cooperation in coming here."

"Insist? On my air-fortress? You've done your duty, Mr. Longman. Let me handle things from here."

Lazarus threw Vasquez an apologetic look and tried to reassure him that everything would be fine. But Vasquez's eyes were outmatched only by the piercing stare of Hok'ee, who seemed to be able to tear holes through him with those black pupils. Lazarus was consumed by an awful feeling of betrayal as he followed General Reynolds to his office.

They passed a platform in the deck that was being raised amid a fug of vapor. On it stood six mechanicals; highly polished, highly equipped war machines painted with Confederate colors. These were no rust-streaked tin cans like the Mecha-guard onboard the *Mary Sue*. This was the new face of war; clean, ruthless and efficient.

"As you can see," said Reynolds standing proudly with his gloved hands behind his back as they watched the mechanicals, "we are equipped to deal with anything that might stand in the way of our pursuit of the golden cities."

"Do you really believe they exist?" Lazarus asked him.

The general looked at him askance. "Got the map here, don't we?"

"It just seems a little unlikely, that's all, General."

"Plenty of treasures have been turned up on this continent and the one south of Mexico. The Spaniards got the Aztec and Inca empires. Now it's our turn to reap this land's wealth that will bring us to further greatness."

"The Aztecs and Incas fell centuries ago," said Lazarus. "This land may have precious few secrets left."

"Nonsense," the general snapped. "White man has barely begun to reap the rewards of this land. The Southern states cannot afford to be shut off from all possibility of expansion by the hostile action of the federal government. We already own Mexico. And we shall push further—south as well as north—have no doubt about that. The tropics are still more or less uncharted. Do you know how much wealth might still be down there, undiscovered by the Spaniards, hidden by steaming jungles and brainless savages? No no, Mr. Longman, we are far from finished with this harvest."

General Reynolds' office was decked out in green velvet with a wide mahogany desk, a fireplace and two studded leather armchairs.

"Now then," said the general as he poured them both some cognac from a decanter. "Let's hear about these adventures you've been having. I received reports that the train from Yuma came into station with two carriages running with blood, and the post office and horse cars cut loose and drifting in the desert. You've got some explaining to do, young man."

The General's reprimand was jovial. He threw himself down into one of the armchairs and indicated to Lazarus to do the same.

"There was something of an altercation on board," he began.

The general hooted. "An 'altercation'? Is that British for a rowdydow?"

"An agent of the Russian Tsar was also looking to apprehend Vasquez and the map."

"Hmm, and hoping to sell him to the Union, is my

thinking."

"Indeed. After the... *rowdydow*, we escaped on horses, taking the Russian with us."

"This Russian fellow fell in with you?" said Reynolds, automatically assuming Katarina was a man.

"I believe they had designs to lure us into the hands of the Unionist rebels." For some reason, Lazarus was very reluctant to tell this man anything about Katarina. Or anything he absolutely didn't have to for that matter. "It certainly turned out that way. We took Vasquez's balloon north and set down at a deserted outpost at the foot of the mountains where Vasquez had some supplies stored."

"I know the one. I'll obliterate that when I have the chance. Have to stop snakes like Vasquez from using our leftovers."

"We set out to retrieve the map from the cave in which Vasquez had secreted it, and then found ourselves betrayed by the Russian and in the hands of the U.P.R."

Lazarus did not give any details about the underground railroad or its location. But the information he had given seemed to satisfy the general, who leaned back in his chair, whistling through his teeth.

"Your story reads like a dime novel. Never trust a Russian, that's what we can learn here."

They had barely tasted their cognac when an eager young sergeant hammered on the door before opening it and hurling up a salute. "An advance party of armed civilians are on the ground northwest from us."

"Rebels?"

"They appear to be, Sir."

Reynolds pounded his fist on the arm of his chair.

"This will be your Unionist partisans, Longman. We'll soon make short work of them!"

Lazarus's stomach lurched as he thought of Katarina on their trail, wandering under the shadow of Reynolds' balloon of terror.

"Follow me," said the general, slamming his glass down on the desk corner as he bolted from the room.

They entered the bridge; a wide observation deck open on all sides. It had two tiers, both with a dizzying array of wheels, instruments, valves and pressure gauges. An officer let the general peer through a mounted telescope. "Has the *Gabriel* finished making its checks?" he asked.

"No sir."

"Then send the *Azrael*. If they are rebels, then Captain Burke has his orders to decimate them."

They watched the *Azrael* inflate its balloons and lift off, drifting away from the *Fort Flagstaff II* towards their target in the distance.

A vision of the smoking ruins of a bombed pueblo flashed through Lazarus's mind. He thought of Katarina down there and her rebel companions; Captain Townsend and Lieutenant Thompson. He wanted to call a halt to the maneuver, but for the life of him couldn't come up with a reasonable explanation. Instead, he was forced to smile and laugh at the jokes of General Reynolds and his officers for the half an hour it took for the *Azrael* to reach its target. The atmosphere was jovial, and it sickened Lazarus to his stomach. He was a military man himself and knew all too well the desensitizing effect of exposure to constant slaughter but having stood face to face with the people down there, it was a bitter pill to swallow.

They watched the *Azrael* discharge its bombs. From

that distance they couldn't see them fall, but they saw them impact; expanding explosions of fire and dust, decimating everything in a mile radius. Lazarus's hands gripped the banister tight enough to make his wrists cramp.

"Well, that's the last of them," said General Reynolds. "Twenty or so less rebels for us to worry about."

"General, I wonder if I may be excused," said Lazarus. "I am tired from my journey and you clearly have much to keep you occupied. Is there a cabin that I may use?"

"Certainly. I'll have a cadet show you to your room. Freshen up, sleep a little if you wish, and then join me at my table for dinner this evening. We must discuss your drop off point. I can arrange for you to take a train to Mississippi, or wherever you are planning to take a steamer back to England."

"That's very kind of you."

Lazarus was shown to his cabin, where he found clean clothes and towels laid out for him. He opened the porthole to let a breeze in and stared at himself in the mirror. He looked a fright. Sweat and dust was plastered to his face, which had sprouted several days' worth of unseemly growth. He looked worse than when Morton had found him reeling drunk in a gutter shortly before he had been given the mission to track down Vasquez. It was a miracle that he had been recognized. Several months of hard drinking and only occasional washing on his journey from South America to the northern continent had taken its toll. There was little left of the neat, professional Englishman who had left London.

Now, he had reverted to that picture of a derelict

drifter, and it brought back bad associations. He decided to do something about it. He washed thoroughly and shaved away the prickly growth but left a moustache that he trimmed with a little pair of gold handled scissors. He put on a clean shirt and collar and glanced briefly at the bed. It looked painfully inviting, but he could not shake his thoughts of Vasquez and Hok'ee in the brig, in irons most likely, and the map to Cibola in the hands of General Reynolds; the terror of the Colorado Plateau.

He returned to the mirror and stared at himself some more as he thought things over. He was so very tired. The streets of London, with the scent of their pies and jellied eels beckoned him. But piercing through that comforting fug of memory was a vision of a lake in the jungle, its waters red, the light of burning homes reflected in its dark depths; reflecting his face, screaming and bloodied. The ruins of that bombed out pueblo flashed through his mind, a striking parallel to the slaughter he had witnessed on the shores of Lake Guatavita. He had no right to return home. Not while a man like General Reynolds was on his way to more slaughter, aided by him. No matter how he looked at it, he would never be done here, he would never be free of his guilt.

Not until he put some wrong things right.

Chapter Eight

In which a battle takes place in the clouds

Lazarus left his cabin and made his way down to the brig, asking for directions along the way. A plan was forming in his mind. He stopped off at the quartermaster and secured two Confederate uniforms in the largest sizes they had. He secreted these behind a boiler pipe in the gangway near the brig before entering.

The jailer was harder to convince than the quartermaster, and rightly so. He was responsible for some very dangerous prisoners and told Lazarus this in no friendly terms. However, Lazarus was prepared for some resistance and his approach was firm from the beginning.

"General Reynolds and I conversed not ten minutes ago," he insisted. "I am his friend and associate and have orders to collect Vasquez and his savage companion personally and escort them to his office for interrogation. I'm sure you understand that they are no ordinary prisoners and this is no ordinary situation."

"Yessir," said the jailer. "They are exceedingly dangerous. A guard of no less than three men is required to transport them."

"Three Americans, I have no doubt," replied Lazarus with a smirk. "I, however, have been trained by the British Army and am more than a match for two greasy bandits." He pulled the flap of his jacket to one side to reveal the Colt Starblazer in its holster.

The jailer gaped at it, and suddenly seemed more cooperative. Soon Lazarus was in the cell that held his companions, a pair of manacles in one hand.

"While I appreciate the notion," said Vasquez once Lazarus had explained his plan, "you can surely understand that I'm a little reserved in trusting you again."

"I appreciate that, Vasquez," said Lazarus. "I made a horrible mistake in bringing you here, and I'm sorry."

"Tell me, did you know this man Reynolds before we arrived here?"

"No. My orders were to turn you over to the nearest governmental fort so long as there was a man there who ranked higher than a captain. I had no idea that I would find a monster such as Reynolds."

"He's a monster, all right."

"I take it you two have a history."

"We three," Vasquez corrected, nodding to Hok'ee, who sat in brooding silence. Lazarus could see the hate in the Navajo's eyes at the mention of the general's name. "It's kind of a long story, but the skinny version is that Reynolds and I were both lieutenants in the corps under General Sibley. Baylor was governor of Arizona then, and he hated the natives with a passion. Once the Union had been pushed out after the victory of the New Mexico Campaign, we were given the job of keeping an eye on the Navajo and other tribes to make sure they didn't get up to any raiding.

"Congress came up with the plan of relocating the Navajo and Mescalero Apaches to a reservation at Bosque Redondo in De Baca County. They were told that it was farmable land where they would live in peace and learn new methods of agriculture. Of course, they didn't want to go. They had their own lands and ways and didn't give a damn what white man thought of their agricultural methods. So the orders came to move them forcibly. I didn't much care for this myself and I wish to God that I had never played my part in it, but I was young and more liable to follow orders then than I am now. So we rounded them up, Reynolds and I and all the other lieutenants under that old drunk Sibley. Sibley wasn't a bad sort really, but totally under the sway of Bastard Baylor. Baylor would have shot every last one of them had it been up to him.

"We could have taken them by airship—it certainly would have been quicker—but there were those who didn't trust natives enough to let them onboard our precious dirigibles. So we walked. Or rather, the Navajo walked. We rode on horseback.

"Damn near nine thousand Navajo were marched at gunpoint for over four hundred miles. About eight hundred of them died on the way, mostly children and the sickly. We didn't have time to bury them. In their language the Navajo call it 'the Long Walk'. After eighteen days we reached Fort Sumner and the promised reservation.

"Right from the get-go I could see that it was never going to work. Navajos and Apaches living side by side? Only a damn-fool congressman from Virginia or Kentucky or some damn place could presume to think they'd put up with each other's company. I'm from Arizona myself, and know that Navajo and Apache are more likely to bury each other than bunk with each other. There were near ten thousand on that reservation. Water was poor, firewood scarce and disease and starvation ran rampant. Not outside of the

Bible have I heard tell of such a hellish place of the damned.

"Raids from the neighboring Comanche were occasional, and the Navajo and Apache raided them back, stirring up more trouble. We deployed the new Mecha-guards to enforce a perimeter around Bosque Redondo. There was no pretense of it being a reservation anymore. It was a prison, pure and simple. The mechanicals were early designs and liable to break down easily, so they needed more or less constant human supervision. We came under attack by a Comanche raiding party one afternoon and we fought them off pretty good, but it was then that I made my discovery. One of the mechanicals had been struck and pulled down by three Comanche. It still had the torn-off limb of one of them in his fist, and blood was plastered to its armor. It'd been pumped with a few shotgun rounds, but it was the tomahawk jammed in its neck that had killed the organic pilot and crippled the machine.

"One of our engineers popped the covering to remove the organic. These boys were expensive things and we couldn't leave it to rust on the plains, but it was no use letting the dead pilot stink things up. We soldiers never really paid much mind to where they got the organics from, but when the engineer removed that scarred plating and we saw the dead Navajo strapped inside with his arms and legs lopped off to make him fit, plugs and tubes coming out of every hole, we realized the true reasoning behind the Long Walk and the hell-hole of Bosque Redondo.

"We rode back to Fort Sumner in silence. I had made up my mind to desert before we even stabled our horses. But I had to know the truth first. There was a laboratory in the bowels of the fort that was off limits to everybody except the eggheads Baylor employed to work on the mechanicals. When I got down there, they were in the process of trying out a new procedure on a Navajo that left no misunderstanding as to why he was chosen for the job. He was huge and was surely a formidable warrior in his own tribe. But Baylor's fruitcakes wanted to 'improve' him. Make him stronger, faster and above all, utterly subservient; a blindly loyal killing machine.

"They had him strapped to a table and his right arm was already gone, sawed off at the elbow. Some mechanical doohickey was bolted onto the bone and they were clearly considering doing the same to his legs. This was the new generation mechanical, much more than an iron suit for a man, but an *iron man*. Hok'ee was the prototype for a whole new mechanical army. Thank God they lost the prototype."

Lazarus gazed from Vasquez to Hok'ee, his eyes wide. "And so you broke him out?"

"That's about the size of it. I shot two scientists and set a fire in that laboratory. There were other horrors there—failed prototypes—things I won't go into 'cause they are in my nightmares too often for me to spend words on them in my waking hours. I unstrapped Hok'ee and found a gun attachment for his arm. They'd given him some practice with his mechanics on the lab's firing range, and he got a whole load more when we left the laboratory. The fire got going wildly, and after we had streaked the walls of the fort red with the blood of anybody who got in our way, we boarded an Interceptor-class balloon and took off to where we could watch the smoke from above. We had a full load of bombs on board, and you can bet we unloaded every last one of them on Fort Sumner.

"The Navajo and the Apaches no doubt saw the smoke from their reservation and took that as the sign to return to their homes. Any mechanicals or humans that were guarding the perimeter were overcome and beaten to death. I might have felt sorry for the old comrades in my unit, but after I had learned what we were fighting for, I was too ashamed and felt I should be down there getting slaughtered with the rest of them. But we'd done our bit, Hok'ee and I, and the Bosque Redondo experiment was over in an afternoon."

"By Jove, there's more to you two than meets the eye," said Lazarus. "So that's how you got the *Santa Bella* and the prices on your heads."

"Yup, the government were none too happy with us, I can tell you. But the damnedest thing is that their most deadly agent was once a friend of mine. Reynolds survived the bombing of Fort Sumner. God knows how he got out alive but get out he did and has been dead set on stringing me up ever since. He was a ruthless son of a bitch when we were in the same unit, but he got even worse after the Bosque Redondo affair. I guess I'm partly to blame for that. Reynolds came from a family of bandits. They got out of the noose by hunting for treasure in Colorado to finance the South. Now Reynolds is playing the same old trick. And they even made him a damned general! He wants Cibola and knows we're the only ones who can take him there."

"Vasquez, you are more of a gentleman than I ever gave you credit for," said Lazarus. "Your story is an inspiration. What do you say we pull off something similar to your antics at Bosque Redondo right now?"

"Well, I suppose you ain't too bad yourself. For a

limey! You got the guard's palm all greased up?"

"The grease in my revolver was all he needed."

"What's the plan?"

"I have uniforms stowed nearby. You can walk out like Confederate soldiers and I'll be your escort. I thought we might take a look at those dirigibles on deck. Maybe take one out to reconnoiter. Under the orders of General Reynolds of course."

"I like your thinking, but what about Hok'ee? No uniform, no matter how fancy, will hide a seven-foot Navajo with a metal elbow."

Lazarus sheepishly admitted that he hadn't thought of that. "I'm afraid that the only way out for Hok'ee is as our prisoner," he said. "We can claim he is accompanying us as he knows the layout of the land and can reveal useful landmarks."

Hok'ee scowled. "No white man will ever put manacles on me again."

"Take it easy, pal," said Vasquez. "He's right. There's no other explanation we can use."

"Then I'll just hold them loosely on my wrists," Hok'ee replied. "Unlocked. I don't want to be chained up when the guns start firing."

"Very well," said Lazarus. "I hope you understand Hok'ee, that I would never wish to see you chained."

Hok'ee grinned that wolfish smile of his. "You say that now, white man…"

The jailer stood well back as Lazarus brought them through, his hand resting on the butt of his pistol. Once they were out on the gangway, Lazarus released Vasquez and gave him his uniform to put on. They swanned out on deck with Hok'ee between them, drawing much more attention than Lazarus was comfortable with.

The *Azrael* had recently landed, and its furnace and boiler were still ticking over. Two soldiers were resupplying its bomb magazine.

"No need for that, my good fellows," said Lazarus striding up to them.

They swiveled to gape at him. Their eyes quickly widened when they saw Hok'ee whose elbow was gripped by Vasquez, keeping the brim of his cap low to shield his eyes.

"We've the general's orders to take her out again on a scouting run to the foot of the mountains," Lazarus continued. "This native here is going to point out some useful landmarks."

"We ain't heard tell of these orders," one of them said. "And only two armed men to pilot her? What if that Injun breaks loose?"

"I'm glad you're so sensitive to the needs of safety," said Lazarus. "It shows me I've picked the right two fellows for the job. My good friend the general, told me to pick out whomever I wanted. Now, prepare this vessel for launch, or whatever you fellows would call it, and we'll be off."

They hustled Hok'ee on board and secured him below deck. Lazarus gave Vasquez and the two soldiers whatever help they needed in preparing for departure. He didn't have to act the ignorant foreigner, for the needs of an airship were truly alien to him. Finally, after what seemed to him an unsubstantiated amount of fussing and checking, they were ready. Vasquez was in the process of casting off the anchor lines when one of the soldiers noticed his empty holster.

"Where's your sidearm, private?" he asked.

Vasquez looked up at him. "Don't need one," he said, and planted his boot squarely in the chest of the young soldier and sent him hurling over the railing to crash to the deck below.

The soldier's companion let out a cry and drew his revolver. Lazarus fired once, the bullet knocking him into a slump at the stairs to the wheelhouse. Together, he and Vasquez lifted the corpse up and tossed it over the side.

"So much for your mission," Vasquez said to Lazarus with a smile. "That'll sure have your government's drawers in a tangle. Welcome to the outlaw's life!"

Hok'ee slammed open the door to below decks and poked his head out. "Am I a free man again?" he asked.

"As free as the day you were born!" cried Lazarus. "Now help us cast off! They're closing in on all sides!"

It was no exaggeration. Alarmed by the shot fired and the thudding of two bodies on the deck, soldiers were converging on the *Azrael*'s dock. Somebody somewhere was ringing an alarm bell.

They began to lift, still in the shadow of *Fort Flagstaff II*'s enormous balloon cluster. As they drifted out over the deck, the desert yawned beneath them and made Lazarus queasy. But the deck of the air fortress began to drift around, following their shadow on the sandy terrain.

"Damn, their captain is quick off the mark!" said Vasquez. "They're already moving after us—the whole goddamned floating fortress! Hok'ee! Start shoveling that mechanite! Full steam!"

The gargantuan air fortress began to lag as the *Azrael* zipped out from under its balloon, but other vessels—the *Gabriel* included—were beginning to take off, and these could match them pace for pace.

Vasquez joined Hok'ee in the engine room and the

two of them shoveled mechanite into the blazing purple furnace so that the sweat ran down them in rivulets. Lazarus busied himself on deck loading the six cannon and fitting new magazines into the deck-mounted dual Jericho Gatling gun.

"They're trying to come across our port bow!" he called down to the engine room.

Hok'ee stormed on deck and set himself to aiming one of the Whitworth guns. Each of the six were on wheeled carriages, mounted on a swivel base for maximum articulation. He trained it on the nearest of the dirigibles and yanked the lanyard. It shot backwards in its tracks and sent its shot roaring through the sky to splinter into the wooden hull of the *Gabriel*.

"We need to aim for the balloons," Lazarus suggested. This earned him a withering look from Hok'ee. "Sorry. I'm sure you'll hit your mark next time."

"Help me reload, Englishman. Then you can aim the next shot."

They opened the smoking breech of the gun and began the process of cleaning and reloading. Lazarus aimed—with Hok'ee moving the carriage for him—and fired. The shot went higher this time and tore through the balloon of the *Gabriel*, causing it to sink instantly as its crew hurried about in a panic.

"Not bad," Hok'ee grudgingly remarked. "For an Englishman."

"Come now, Hok'ee, these guns were invented by an Englishman! And I've had plenty of experience firing them in the Ashanti Campaign." A return shot tore through the railings and showered them in splinters. "Bloody hell that was close!"

Vasquez yelled at them from below. "What the hell

are you two clowns playing at? Can't you see one of them has crept up on our starboard bow? At this rate we'll collide with it!"

Hok'ee made for the wheelhouse to correct their course, while Lazarus strapped himself into the Jericho gun. Much like the one Hok'ee had attached to his arm, its twin barrel clusters had an automatic cranking mechanism leaving Lazarus's hands free to grasp the two handles.

Once he had trained the crosshairs on the balloon of the approaching ship, he squeezed both triggers and sent a hail of death its way. The distance was too great for it to do much damage, but he managed to pepper the hull of the ship.

"Hok'ee, bring us in closer!"

"Closer?" he heard Vasquez yell, but Hok'ee understood and obeyed without question. It was a dangerous gamble, but it was the only way to get the final balloon off their trail.

They drifted towards the path of their pursuer and Lazarus winced as a shot from its bow tore into their own balloon.

"That's done it!" said Vasquez, his head poking out of the engine room. "We're going down unless I do something fast!"

"Then do it, man!" Lazarus shouted. The pursuing ship was within a decent range now, and he squeezed the triggers again, holding them down as the ammunition ran through the chambers like a mountain stream. The bullets made Swiss cheese of the enemy's balloon, cutting it to ribbons and sending it hurtling towards the ground faster than the *Gabriel*.

"Great shot, limey!" yelled Vasquez. "Now if only we can stay afloat long enough to get out of the reach of any ground party they send to recover our wreckage…"

Lazarus unbuckled the straps and climbed out from behind the red-hot smoking guns. "Is it really as bad as all that?"

"We're losing helium fast. All I can do is open all tanks and pump her full of it. It won't take us far, but it might carry us over the mountain range. We'll have to lighten the load as best we can."

"Right. We won't be needing these cannons anymore."

"That's the ticket. You and Hok'ee get to it. I'll handle the piloting."

As a pair, Lazarus and Hok'ee wrestled the guns out of their carriages and tossed them overboard, followed by the carriages themselves. The Jericho gun went too, and Lazarus swore as he blistered his hand when he accidently touched one of the barrels. Vasquez had opened all valves and their descent had slowed a bit, but they were still dropping. Lazarus went below and looked for anything that wasn't bolted down. Chairs, tables, pots and pans all went the way of the guns, littering the mountain range that looked ready to start tickling their bellies. Vasquez was steering the craft wildly, following canyons and passes as if he was following a map.

"Where exactly are you taking us, Vasquez?" asked Lazarus, stepping into the wheelhouse.

"Only place I can think of where a ground party won't reach us."

Lazarus peered at the red mountains. Beyond them was the State of Deseret. Below them, the Colorado River diverged into its tributary of the Little Colorado, surrounded by stacks of limestone. In this natural 'Y' shape lay the badlands of the Painted Desert; Navajo lands.

"We're going to Hok'ee's people?"

"Not quite so far as that," said Vasquez. "Not enough helium. There's one other place in the mountains where we can set down, though I'm not sure what sort of a welcome we might get. They ain't much used to white folks. It ain't on any map, you see. Well apart from one, that is."

"You don't mean…"

"Yep. We're about to take you to Cibola."

"You mean it really does exist? You've been there?"

"Only once and only for a very short time. Like I said, they don't much like white folks."

"They? Who lives there?"

"Pueblo people. Much like the Zuni and the Hopi, but they're their own tribe. A mountain people more or less untouched for centuries. You'll understand why soon enough. Hold on tight. It's going to be a bumpy landing."

They came so close to scraping their keel on the mountain ridges, that Lazarus was about ready to start ripping up the decking and hurling it overboard to lighten the load some more.

"We're almost there," said Vasquez. "Get your head down, I don't think we're quite gonna make this one!"

He was right. Lazarus was hurled off his feet as the keel struck an outcropping and sent the craft spinning around in dizzying circles. Vasquez desperately tried to regain control, but the wheel spun like a demon as the little craft was swallowed by a vast open basin. Lazarus caught flashes of green forest and turquoise water, vividly contrasting against the dusty reds and oranges of the arid mountains and thought he must be hallucinating as they went down, down, deep into another world.

Chapter Nine

In which Cibola is seen for the first time by an Englishman

Lazarus spat the blood from his mouth and rolled over. He could hear Vasquez struggling to do the same. Hok'ee was hunched over the wheel, and the way he eased himself off it and slumped to the floor with a groan made Lazarus wonder if he hadn't broken a rib or two. The floor of the wheelhouse was tilted at a dizzying angle, and Lazarus found it hard to get to his feet. All the windows but one were broken, and the branches of pines had been thrust through several, curling up under the ceiling.

Vasquez staggered over to the door and opened it. Lazarus tried to follow, disliking the way the airship bobbed and bounced with every footstep. The ground was many feet below them, and the *Azrael* teetered precariously in the branches of two close trees.

"Don't nobody move," said Vasquez in a whisper, as if even a loud voice might dislodge them and send them crashing downwards.

"We'll have to step out, one by one, as softly as possible," urged Lazarus. "Another minute in this thing might be the death of us all."

"You first," said Vasquez, apparently preferring to remain in the trees for a bit than meet the ground prematurely.

Lazarus moved as if he were an old man, slowly easing himself over the railing, feeling the burn in his arm muscles as he lowered himself into the branches of the tree. He began to climb, but quickly ran out of branches and had to wrap his arms and legs around its trunk and slide down in grating agony before he felt the reassuring needle-blanketed ground beneath his feet. Hok'ee came next, in double time, more eager to meet the ground than even Lazarus had been.

"I'll toss down some things we might need!" called down Vasquez.

Down came a cascade of tools, ammunition and medical supplies as well as food rations and full canteens.

"Now for the mechanite!"

"What do we need that for?" Lazarus called up.

"It's value! Might be able to trade it with anybody we might meet."

"Don't try to reach the boiler room," Lazarus cried. "It's folly!"

But Vasquez's head had already disappeared. The *Azrael* jolted sickeningly and his pale face reemerged. "You're right. We won't need that mechanite." He came down quickly, slipping and sliding like a drunken bear. "Lord, I'm glad to be out of there."

As soon as he had finished his exclamation, the *Azrael* slipped several feet, with a great tearing sound and a shower of needles.

They stood on a forested slope that led down to the shores of an enormous lake. Towering mountains rose behind them and ringed them on all sides, enveloping the lake and meeting in the distance in a haze of purple. Patches of green streaked the feet of the mountains, making a stark contrast to the fiery red rock. Right up to the edge of the lake crept the thick forest of firs, junipers and ponderosa pines. It was a genuine lost world; a timeless land set amid the arid deserts and barren canyons of Arizona.

"This whole rock basin must act as a rain trap," said Lazarus, looking about at the crawling tendrils that stretched up the slopes of the mountains like a frayed green carpet. "That's how such a fertile land can survive surrounded by desert."

The three of them stood for a while and admired the view. There was no doubt in Lazarus's mind that, golden cities or no, they had truly found the land of Cibola.

They made their way down into the forested basin. The going was tough, and every so often one of them would put a foot wrong and go sliding down on his rear in a cascade of pine needles and dust. No paths showed themselves and they saw no dwellings or any sign of human habitation. A large rattlesnake hissed its warning at them from nearby, and Lazarus proceeded more carefully, remembering the array of deadly animals that America held in its bosom.

The sound of rushing water reached their ears and they made for it with renewed vigor. At last, they emerged on the edge of a glorious pool at the foot of a waterfall. Hot, sweaty and thirsty, the three of them stripped off and plunged into the cool depths of the pool, drinking up the fresh water. They splashed about for a while, letting the moisture wash away the dirt and soak into their tired bodies. They were so wrapped up in their enjoyment that it took them a while to realize that they were being watched.

Upon the side of the pool stood six men. Their skin was coppery like Hok'ee's, but their clothing and ornamentation was wholly unlike the Navajo. They wore simple garments of animal skin and cloth and carried stone-headed weapons. Their hair was extraordinary. In every case it was bound and tied into various sculptures and woven around ornaments of bone and colored stones. They were tall too, far taller than was usual in Native American peoples.

They had been fishing and carried an enormous catch between them on poles. Their leader barked out something and thrust his fishing spear three times in some sort of offensive gesture. Hok'ee replied in a dialect that Lazarus assumed was Zuni or Hopi or one of the other pueblo languages, for it certainly wasn't Navajo.

The leader beckoned them to come out of the pool, which they did, Lazarus and Vasquez acutely aware of their nakedness. The hunters came forward and inspected them, further ruining their dignity with prods and pokes as if they were men from the moon. Clearly, white men were an exceedingly rare sight in this basin. They paid Hok'ee's skin color less attention but compensated for this with great interest in his metal implants.

Once he was satisfied, the leader of the hunting party bade them dress and follow them. His troop picked up their fish and escorted them through the forest. Lazarus was uneasy. He had no idea where they were being taken or even if these new friends of theirs had good intentions towards them or ill. He guessed that their village was not far, for none of the hunters were equipped for a long journey.

They followed the river, crossing it twice as it twisted and curved through the forest on its way to the lake, and ascended a steep incline that took them up and out of the greenery to a red rocky hillside. They heard the sound of voices; children playing and a woman singing. Stairs cut into the rock led up to a dizzying height. Below them stretched a vast mesa of fertile crops.

They emerged onto a wide ledge that fell back beneath a bulging overhang. Into this natural recess, the tribe had built their village. Some dwellings were cut into the rock, while others had been built of stone and logs. Ladders led up to flat roofs and small, square windows peeped out at them. All about were people. Women ground corn and shaped pots, blackening them in fires. Men cut stone tools and were engaged in the hauling up of water from the river below using a pulley system. Baskets of corn and squash came up from the irrigated mesa. Other women plastered houses, while turkeys strutted about with proud dignity at their freedom to roam.

Lazarus realized that it was not just the ones sent out as hunters and warriors who were the tallest. All of these people—*Cibolans*, he supposed they could be called—were large, much larger than the average Englishman. He put this down to their diet, which must be a vast improvement on the diets of their Navajo or Hopi cousins due to the lush fertility of their land. They also wore garments of fine cotton, hinting at an abundance of that material down in the valley.

The new arrivals had attracted a good deal of attention. A crowd had gathered about them and were talking excitedly in their own language while the lead hunter tried to tell them his story. An elderly man wearing ornamentations of jade and shell came towards them. The crowd parted respectfully to let him through. Lazarus put him down as some sort of healer or medicine man. After being examined by this old man and questioned at length, they were led away into a part of the village complex. Hok'ee translated what had passed between them. "His name is Tohotavo. He is the priest for the clan. We are being taken before their chief. His name is Eototu."

In the dim interior of the pueblo, it took a while for their eyes to grow accustomed to the light that streamed in through the square window. Logs crackled in a corner fireplace. Benches had been carved out of the rock of one wall and constructed of flat stones on the other. The stream of Cibolans that filed into the room sat down on these benches, eager to witness the audience with the chief.

Eototu came in from an adjoining room, with his family in tow. He was tall, proud and strong, clothed in colorful threads tied over one shoulder. He swept those majestically aside as he seated himself at the head of the room. An in-depth interrogation was conducted of the hunters and of Hok'ee. Hok'ee then conversed with Vasquez in Navajo.

"They ain't pleased to see us," Vasquez told Lazarus. "Eototu has heard the tale of us from the last time we dropped in. He thinks our flying machines are a demonic menace."

"What exactly happened here the last time you 'dropped in'," Lazarus asked, growing increasingly nervous. "I think it's about time you told me."

Vasquez sighed. "Not much and that's the truth. We came here and realized that there was no gold to be found, and so we left. We only stayed a couple of days and even that was more than we were welcome to. These people just want to be left alone. They've got their own private slice of paradise here and nobody's got the right to take it from them. That's why they're so secretive."

A sudden feeling of guilt and impending doom stirred in Lazarus. He spoke in a hurried voice, "We have to warn them! We have to tell them that General Reynolds is coming with an army of flying machines, and when he finds that there is no gold here he'll be enraged."

"Don't I know it? I wish we didn't have to land in this valley but it was the only option open to us." He brought himself to Hok'ee's attention and told him in Navajo to relay the warning to Eototu.

Hok'ee did so, and if the Cibolans had been angry at them before they were doubly so now. Lazarus couldn't blame them. They had crashed into their garden of Eden like the harbingers of the apocalypse, heralding an enemy a thousand times more technologically advanced in warfare than they were.

"Tell them they must evacuate, Hok'ee," said Lazarus. "They cannot hope to stand against Reynolds. We will help them flee and if there are any other villages in this valley, then they too must be warned."

Hok' ee looked at him curiously and relayed the message. It had little effect on the chief and there was a great deal of angry murmuring throughout the room. Evidently, the Cibolans were insulted by the idea of fleeing. An instruction was given to them by Eototu.

"He says we are the ones who must leave, and immediately," said Vasquez. "We can stay here for the night and they will give us food and provisions to take with us, but we must fix the *Azrael* and take off tomorrow."

"We don't have the helium," said Lazarus.

"Hok'ee tried to tell them that, but they don't

understand. As far as they're concerned we are sorcerers and if we flew in here by magic then we can damn well fly out by magic."

"Reynolds will be here in less than a day. We must convince them!"

"Sorry, limey. They ain't buying it. We've been given our marching orders and I think we'd better take them. These folks aren't the ones to say no to. We'll get our vittles and some shuteye and then God knows. We'll probably spend the rest of our days wandering through the forests. But we've done all we can here."

Lazarus shut his eyes tight in frustration. They were led away to the home of Tohotavo the priest, where his wife was preparing their meal. A young member of Eototu's family, whom Lazarus assumed was one of his daughters, accompanied them. She was a pretty young girl with hair bound up in buns on either side of her head; a style he remembered usually signified an unmarried girl in the Hopi clans, and assumed it meant something similar in Cibolan culture.

They were fed a meal of squash, beans and flakes of a corn paste spread very thin and baked crispy in the oven. Tohotavo and the girl remained with them. The old priest was genuinely interested in everything Hok'ee had to tell him, while the girl was wholly taken with his maimed arm which she touched occasionally, fascinated by the metal implants that protruded from its stump. He told her the story of how he came to look that way. She watched him with bulging eyes as he related the tale, and Lazarus wondered if she was shocked, appalled or even believed him at all.

"Her name is Kokoharu," Hok'ee explained. "She is one of Eototu's daughters and is an apprentice to Tohotavo. He teaches her medicine and healing, as well as the ways of the spiritual world."

"Please try and warn them again, Hok'ee," said Lazarus. "Perhaps these two will understand the danger. Armed men will be coming here very soon looking for gold. When they don't find it, who knows what will happen?"

Hok'ee nodded and spoke to them. "They are a stubborn and fearless people," he said after a while. "They understand the danger but would not dishonor their ancestors by fleeing. They will fight even though they may die."

Lazarus set his bowl down, his appetite gone. They were shown to beds of turkey feathers, and with the embers of the fire glowing like serpent's eyes in the darkness, they lay down to sleep.

Chapter Ten

In which the first war for Cibola begins

Lazarus's troubled dreams kept him asleep longer than his comrades. When he finally woke, he found Vasquez and Hok'ee shoveling down a breakfast of pine nuts and cold fish as if they were in a great hurry. Outside the window he could hear the Cibolans talking excitedly and calling from one end of the village to the other.

"The clan is preparing for war," Vasquez explained. "They say a great force has landed in the west not far from where we set down. I'm betting Reynolds has found the *Azrael* and knows we're here."

"Preparing for war?" Lazarus asked, astounded. "We must stop them! They'll be obliterated!"

"Love to agree with you, but you heard them last night. They won't accept anything less than an honorable death. We're going to head out with the first scouting party and assess their advance. The forests will slow the Confeds down, especially if they've got mechanicals. Good thing I brought a telescope from the *Azrael*. It'll come in handy."

Lazarus crammed down some nuts and fish and washed it down with water from a clay jug. They emerged from the pueblo to see that a thick mist had cloaked the treetops below them like a carpet of cotton. Warriors were assembling in units to descend the cliff and into the mist. They carried clubs embedded with sharpened chunks of obsidian, and Lazarus realized that the Cibolans did not use iron or any other metal. They were so cut off from the rest of the American tribes that they still fashioned tools and weapons from stone.

The scouting party set out and descended the steep slope into the forest. They followed the feet of the red cliffs as they curved around to the south, towards the location where the *Azrael* had crashed. When they neared it, their leader held up his hand for halt, and all crouched down with an efficiency that would have made Lazarus's old drill instructor blush with pride.

Hands gripped weapons tightly as they crept forward. The pines grew thick on the slopes and screened them from view.

"That fella must have the eyes of a hawk to see anything," said Vasquez. "Either that or he's just fooling around. Let's see what he thinks of my telescope." The bandit shambled forward on his haunches to the leader's side and snapped open his telescope. All eyes were upon him as he peered through this strange contraption. He passed it to the leader to have a look.

The effect was comical. The leader nearly toppled backwards at having the view suddenly explode in his eye, and he almost cast the thing away as an evil object. But the usefulness of such an item quickly became apparent to him and he held on to it, scrambling further up the slope to get a less obstructed view.

"I think you can say goodbye to your telescope," said Lazarus, once Vasquez returned to his side.

"He can have it. These poor bastards are going to need every trick in the book if they are to stand a chance against what lies beyond those trees."

"Oh?"

"Reynolds is there, alright. I didn't see him but there's enough of his war machinery down there. They've had to cut down plenty of trees to make space for it all. Three dirigibles, an army of Mecha-warriors, not to mention regular infantry all polishing their rifles. They've got digging machines, explosives, steam-powered tree harvesters; the works. They could level this valley with all that junk."

Hok'ee grumbled something in Navajo, and Lazarus needed no translation. "Damn the bastard," he agreed.

Lazarus was pleased to find that the leader of the scouting party was not reckless enough to launch an immediate attack, and soon they were heading back up the ridge towards the village. Their news was received in severe silence. Their world was under attack and something had to be done. The warriors started preparing en masse for battle.

"While the warriors head down into the valley to fight Reynolds," Hok'ee explained, "Tohotavo and Kokoharu will escort the women, the children and the elderly to the northern city. I have spoken with him and we are to help them."

Lazarus glanced over to where Kokoharu was helping another woman lift an elderly man onto a bearer of branches. "The going will be slow," he said. "Must we descend into the forests?"

"No. The way lies along the mountain ridge. It will not take more than a day to reach the northern city. But the going will be single file in some parts."

"How many of these cities are there, Hok'ee?"

"Four for each direction of the compass, and three

down in the valley representing up, down and center. Seven in total. Seven cities for the seven directions in the spiritualism of the pueblo peoples."

With the number seven ringing in his ears, Lazarus went to help Kokoharu in the preparation of the elderly and sick for the journey and together, through the use of sign language, they worked out a system for travelling. If they were to be going single file, he signed to her, then they must be as efficient as possible and stay close together so nobody straggled. She nodded her agreement.

There came a great wailing from outside, and they went to the doorway to look. The warriors were setting out, accompanied by the cries and blessings of their women and children. The faces of the warriors had been rubbed with the ground paste from the flower the Spanish call 'yerba del manso' and designs in black iron and manganese ore covered their bodies, done by the hand of Tohotavo as a blessing and protection against harm. To Lazarus they already looked like ghosts as they marched off to their fate and he had to turn away from the door and busy himself to avoid looking on their ashen faces.

Vasquez and Hok'ee were busy carrying food and supplies from the storage huts and preparing them for transport. The Cibolans possessed no mules or other pack animals, and so all supplies had to be carried by the strongest of the refugees. Lazarus went to find them to discuss who should carry the disabled and who the supplies. He found Vasquez at the foot of a ladder, conversing with a Cibolan in a similar system of gesturing and pointing.

"Where's Hok'ee?" he asked Vasquez.

"Isn't he with you?"

"No, I thought he was helping you with the supplies."

"Haven't seen him in a while."

Lazarus was aware of Kokoharu standing behind him. He turned and saw her face beset with worry. She had evidently understood their concern. "Do you know where he has gone, Kokoharu?" he asked her.

She turned and took off at a run, making for one end of the village. Lazarus ran after her and heard her asking questions of many women. Some shrugged, some shook their heads, while others nodded and pointed at the trail of dust left by the tramping feet of the recently departed warriors. Lazarus did not require Kokoharu's dismayed words and gestures to understand what had happened.

"He did what?" exclaimed Vasquez when Lazarus informed him.

"I can't understand it either," said Lazarus. "Hok'ee always seemed to me to be the most logical and brutally realistic of men. Why he felt the need to join these people on their suicide mission is beyond me."

"You don't know him like I do. Everything he does he does out of passion. Passion rules his life and logic occasionally goes down the can. He feels a kinship with these people—stronger than I can explain to you. It's so strong he's decided to die with them."

"Are we too late to catch up with him and change his mind?"

"We might catch up with him, but it's the changing of his mind that's likely to present a problem."

They went to Tohotavo. They let Kokoharu explain the situation and then Lazarus, in a series of mimes and hand gestures, explained their plan. The old priest seemed reluctant. He spoke in a slow voice, and

Lazarus imagined that he was voicing concerns that should the two of them go tearing after their friend they would be leaving two less people to carry supplies and wounded to the northern city.

But it was Kokoharu who convinced him. She was so upset at Hok'ee's actions that tears threatened to run down her cheeks. But she held them in check, speaking respectfully to her mentor, eventually winning him around. Lazarus had no idea what she said, but it must have been something powerful. Tohotavo nodded sagely and made some hand motions to bless all three of them. Kokoharu, it seemed, was to be their guide in catching up with the warriors.

They struggled to keep up with her lithe form as she leapt through the forests, ducking branches and hopping over fallen trunks. The carpet of pine needles dampened the sound of their running.

There came the sound of gunfire up ahead, and he recognized the booming of Golgotha rifles and the *pump-pump-pump* of Jerichos. They were near the river that fell into the rock pool where the hunting party had found them the day previously.

"For God's sake, slow down!" he cried out, knowing that it was futile. Not only did Kokoharu not understand English, but she was as possessed by a demon as she led them closer and closer to the battle.

"We're going to run right out into the crossfire if we're not careful!" warned Vasquez.

But their lack of faith in their guide was unwarranted, as Kokoharu slid to a sudden halt at an outcropping of pines that hung above the rushing river. Here, screened by the trees, they could see the battle without being seen themselves.

The river was the border between two sides. On

their side the Cibolans were massed, hooting war-cries and occasionally darting into the waters to shoot a volley of arrows at the enemy. These missiles either fell short or bounced harmlessly off the iron armor of the mechanicals that stomped about on the other side, ripping the air with bursts of Jericho fire.

Lazarus could see Eototu, his most prized warriors clustered around him, preparing to make a charge across the river. Hok'ee wasn't with them.

"They're fools to try it!" he said.

"Rage makes men foolish," said Vasquez. "And Hok'ee has more than his share of rage. I wouldn't doubt that in his mind his hatred of Reynolds and the C.S.A. trumps all the rest of it."

"All the rest of what?"

"Never mind. I'm mighty glad this little wildcat here was prepared to take us to him. I just can't let him throw his life away like this."

"Yes, I think she has taken quite a liking to our friend."

They watched with sickened hearts as Eototu led the charge into the river. The water slowed them down, and gunfire from the opposite bank tore into their ranks. Soon the river ran red and only half of the warriors emerged on the other side, scrambling up the bank and continuing towards the enemy.

Eototu, for the moment, remained alive, and Lazarus saw the look in his daughter's eyes. She mourned for him as the Cibolans vanished into the trees to engage the enemy. She brushed a single tear away from her eye, as if accepting that this was the fate that was written for her father.

They climbed down to the riverbank and followed it, as more and more warriors splashed across, inspired by their chief's courageous lead. Further downstream they found another battle had already taken place, which must have preceded Eototu's wild charge. Between ten and fifteen Cibolan warriors had attacked a squad of infantry that had attempted to cross the river in the wake of one of their mechanicals. The great iron warrior was face down in the river with a war club embedded in its spinal column, the blood of its organic pilot flowing away in pink tendrils, steam billowing up from its dampened furnace. Standing over it, wrestling the Jericho gun from its arm, was Hok'ee.

His comrades were whooping and yelling in the ecstasy of slaughter as they tore apart the Confederate troops who, now without their mechanical companion, were all but naked in the face of the ferocious warriors. Their Enfield rifles were useless at such close range and, although some were able to get a few shots off with their revolvers, they fell beneath the pounding of the reddened war clubs.

Hok'ee had succeeded in detaching the Jericho gun from the fallen mechanical and had fitted it to his own arm. The Cibolans went wild as he let off an experimental burst and cheered uproariously.

As they waded through the river towards him, Kokoharu let forth a blistering volley of words in her language which momentarily stunned the hero in the making. Vasquez threw a wink at Lazarus. "I think Hok'ee just got read the riot act by a woman! Hey, Hok'ee! You gonna take on Reynold's whole army with that thing?"

Hok'ee glared at his friend and shouted something in Navajo. He would stoop to no white man's tongue now that vengeance was within his reach.

"We ain't going back without you, pal," Vasquez

responded. "It's death for all of us here or life for all of us back there. You decide."

Something else decided for all of them as a round from an Enfield tore through the breast of one of the warriors standing near Hok'ee. The shot had been meant for him and he whirled, decimating a thicket on the far bank with three short bursts from his Jericho. A Confederate slumped out of the foliage, his face and body a ruin of bloody holes and torn flesh. More rifle shots cracked out. Lazarus drew his Starblazer and searched for cover as Hok'ee and his warriors stormed the bank.

Up to their chests in the cold mountain river and with their backs to a boulder around which the water flowed, Lazarus, Vasquez and Kokoharu peeped out to see the Cibolans entering the trees and heard the burst of Hok'ee's gun and several Confederate rifles.

"Goddamn that lunatic!" cursed Vasquez. "He's gonna get us all killed."

"Come on," Lazarus said, his gun held ready. "Let's try again. But if he still won't listen then I think we should return Kokoharu to her people and do the best we can for them. There's no stopping Hok'ee if this is what he really wants."

With the enemy wholly taken up by the advancing Cibolans, there was nobody to fire upon them as they crossed the rest of the river and waded up the bank. In the shade of the trees they entered a world of gunfire, screams and shouts of anger that seemed all the louder within the muted silence of the forest.

They had barely gone more than twenty paces into the trees when the first of the Cibolans came running in the opposite direction. Something beyond the trees had smashed the fight from them and made them reconsider their advance. Bursts of gunfire ripped through the foliage and two of the fleeing natives fell, their chests torn open by bullets. The massive figure of Hok'ee bounded through the trees, his great corded muscles straining, and his damp skin plastered with the blood of close combat. He saw Vasquez and yelled at him in Navajo.

"There's too many of them!" Vasquez explained. "They've got more mechanicals than we've ever seen. It's hopeless!"

"And how many had to die to learn what we've been trying to tell them all along!" yelled Lazarus. He was livid.

They fell back to the river, with the forest behind them going up in shattered splinters and flames as the war machines of the C.S.A. advanced. They had made it to the rocks in the center of the river before the Confederates emerged from the tree line and began firing once more. Hok'ee turned and fired back, prompting more of his warriors to make another stand.

"No!" cried Lazarus. "We must keep retreating!"

Nobody was listening. Hok'ee continued to pump bullets into the faces of the advancing enemy. When one band of ammunition was used up, he slotted in another he had looted from the downed mechanical and continued firing.

Confederate soldiers in their uniforms waded into the river, firing with rifles and revolvers. The Cibolans ran to meet them, hacking and chopping with their war clubs but there were too many of them. Soon the river ran red with Cibolan blood. All along the river it was the same story; natives fleeing from the trees and trying to cross the river, with the invaders firing at their backs, felling them by the score.

Lazarus's head swam as he felt a civilization and a people die around him. *This couldn't be happening again! It just couldn't!* He was aware of Kokoharu running past him, and he called to her. She didn't heed him, so he called again and only then did he realize that he was calling the wrong name; the name of a different girl from another time and another continent.

He fired again and again at the enemy until his gun clicked empty. He wished for more cartridges. There were almost no Cibolans left now, and the river was choked with their bodies. Only Hok'ee stood, like an oak in the storm, the bloody waters lapping around his knees as he kept on firing, the barrels of his gun glowing red hot. The Confederates were holding back and calling for more mechanicals to be brought forward. Lazarus seized his chance.

"It's over, Hok'ee! You've done all you can! There's nobody left but the women and children. Come back with us now. Come back with Kokoharu and help protect her people!"

The big warrior turned and stared at him with livid eyes that pulsed through the mask of sweat and hair and blood. He seemed to breathe his first lungful in a long time. Then he nodded.

Chapter Eleven

An unexpected homecoming

They hurried back through the forest, following Kokoharu's lead. She claimed to know a shortcut through the basin that would put them on the trail of the refugees without having to return to the western city.

The forests grew thicker and Lazarus was thankful for this, imagining the Confederates struggling to find their way and having to cut a path for their war machines. Cotton grew like snow in summer, and the air danced in the heat.

They passed close to the edge of the lake that sat in the bottom of the basin, formed by the runoff from the rain. The enormity of made Lazarus reluctantly think of Lake Guatavita. There were islands out in its centre; rocky pinnacles with trees on them. He wondered if these held the cities named after the directions 'up', 'down' and 'center' that supposedly lay in the valley and thought to put the question to Hok'ee but they were short of time and breath.

They caught up with the train of refugees, who were alarmed by the sight of Hok'ee, plastered in blood and swinging a huge metal attachment to his arm. They sought out Tohotavo. The priest did not ask them of the battle or what had become of their chief, Eototu. He did not need to. The look of pain in Kokoharu's eyes told the whole story. They continued onwards in silence.

The northern city was much like the western one. Lazarus imagined the eastern and southern ones also sat high up on the cliffs that ringed the lake like points on a compass, peering down onto their sister cities in the basin. A party of warriors was waiting for them at the top of the winding stairs. Tohotavo talked with them, and they were admitted into the village. Lazarus, Vasquez and Hok'ee caused astonishment similar to that of their arrival in the western city, but on a lesser scale due to the gravity of the situation.

While the refugees were given food and water in the nearest homes, Tohotavo, Kokoharu and the outlanders were ushered into the chief's audience. It was a room much like Eototu's, hung with woven patterns and smoky from the burning mesquite logs.

The chieftain was a large man, even for Cibolan standards. His face was wide and framed by black hair that spilled down over massive shoulders nearly to his navel. At his side sat his wife; a stunningly beautiful woman with cold, hard eyes and hair bound in some intricate style that Lazarus did not even try to guess the meaning of. The eyes of the royal couple swept the newcomers and then, when they saw Hok'ee, the both nearly leapt upright.

The chief said something in a loud, commanding voice, to which Hok'ee answered. The woman also spoke, but Hok'ee kept his eyes fixed on the chief, refusing to look at her. Lazarus couldn't work out if everybody else in the room found this severely disrespectful.

"Any idea what's going on?" he asked Vasquez. It was probably a silly question, for Vasquez spoke as much Cibolan as he did, but the bandit appeared to be following the exchange between Hok'ee and the royal couple with somber understanding.

"The chieftain's name is Mankanang," Vasquez replied. "His wife is Xuthala. I think Tohotavo has told them of the invasion from the west, but they seem more interested in Hok'ee."

"How do you know enough Cibolan to pick out their names?" Lazarus asked him.

"I don't. This was the village we came to when we arrived here before. Mankanang was the chief who ordered us to leave and to never come back. And here we are again."

Mankanang gave an order to some of his warriors who loitered in the shadows. They came forward, hands gripping war clubs, as if to take Hok'ee into custody. Tohotavo stepped forward and spoke fast and passionately. Lazarus believed he was telling Mankanang of the Navajo's courageous efforts to defend the western city. Kokoharu also gave her own testimony, no doubt using her status as daughter of a fellow chief who had fallen in battle alongside this brave outlander. Mankanang scowled. He had heard them out. He ordered the warriors to fall back but remained skeptical.

"Well I'll be damned," said Vasquez. "The old bastard has a sympathetic bone in his body after all. I thought old Hok'ee's days were up, and ours too into the bargain. But I guess Mankanang just couldn't go through with it, no matter how much they hate each other."

"What are you talking about?" Lazarus asked. "You speak as if they know each other intimately."

"Hok'ee is Mankanang's brother."

"His brother? You mean Hok'ee is a Cibolan?" Lazarus was flabbergasted and desperately needed this explained, but there was no time for Mankanang was giving a speech. Apparently, there was to be food as painted bowls of squash, beans, corn and venison were brought in and set down on woven mats. They all sat down in a circle around the walls of the chamber and tucked in. Lazarus was ravenous, and hurriedly pushed down the first few mouthfuls of food before he pressed Vasquez for more information.

"It's a long story, pal, and not one that Hok'ee likes to tell often. He told it to me not long after we busted out of Fort Sumner and has never spoken of it since. I picked up more of the tale when we came here the first time. His real name is Pahanatuuwa, and he's not of the Navajo but of this valley. He and Mankanang grew up in one of the other pueblos. Hok'ee—Pahanatuuwa I should say—was the lady-killer of the pair. He was in love with a chief's daughter from another tribe. The Cibolans are matrilineal. That means the royal line passes through the women and they never marry a man from the same clan."

"Much like the Hopi," said Lazarus.

"Yeah. Well, the chiefs in this valley are not born royal. They marry into the royal families. They still do the ordering about, but it's their wives who are the real sovereigns. You might have noticed that the homes here are the property of the women. They are in charge of their upkeep and their husbands are more like guests in them. So, Pahanatuuwa was all set to marry this girl and become a chief. Only then, the hussy goes and takes up with somebody else and the marriage is off. You know Hok'ee has a nasty temper, so he kicks up a ruckus and gets himself exiled."

"Poor Hok'ee—I mean Pahanatuuwa," said Lazarus, eyeing their companion, who was letting Kokoharu serve him some more food. "It hardly seems fair."

"He got the shaft, no doubt about it," Vasquez went on. "Anyway, that's when he left the valley and took up with the Navajo. They gave him a new name and a new life, and pretty soon they got caught up in the war and that's where I met up with him. The poor fella had lost everything for a second time, with all his Navajo friends dead from the Long Walk or from their internment at Bosque Redondo. I figured he'd be happy enough living the life of an outlaw bandit with me for a while. I ain't got no family either so we were a deuce, or so I thought. I never much cared where I came from and I guessed he never did either. But deep down, all he could think about was the woman he had loved and the home he had lost. That's when he got the bright idea of treasure hunting.

"You see, the Cibolans were aware that somebody had made a map to their valley of Eden and weren't too keen on anybody else finding it. Whoever had made the map—Estevanico is my guess—took it with them when they left, all those years ago. The Cibolans wanted it returned. So, Hok'ee was dead-set on finding this map and taking it back here as a peace offering. I figure he hoped to win his way back into the tribe and win over the gal he had lost or something. As for me, as soon as I heard that there was a map to Cibola, I thought the Lord had sent me an all-paid fare to riches and glory. I didn't need any convincing.

"So we found the map after many adventures which I won't go into right now, and flew into this valley expecting to be hailed as heroes. Brother, were we wrong. Hok'ee had already explained to me by that point that there was no gold here, so I wasn't so disappointed when we landed, but the Cibolans were mighty disappointed to see us, especially as we had that damned map with us. We were told to hand it over so that it could be destroyed. They were worried that we had shown it to every white man alive. Hok'ee had another of his stomping fits and told them that as he had found the map it was his, and he wasn't going to leave it here with a bunch of ingrates who wouldn't accept him. If I had known any better, I would have convinced him to toss the useless thing into the lake down there and let that be an end to it.

"But we flew on out of here with our map and found another safe place to bury it. We should have destroyed it ourselves, but we were so high and mighty that we thought we knew best and weren't about to throw away our only link to the Land of the Seven Cities, however lacking in wealth they were. Not that we really considered selling it, for to do that would mean the death of everybody here, as we're witnessing right now. I don't know what we planned to do with it, really. All we knew was that it was ours and we were going to keep it hidden."

"Just a minute," said Lazarus. "When you agreed to hand the map over to either Katarina or myself, did you have any intention of keeping up your end of the bargain?"

Vasquez grinned around a mouthful of venison. "Nope. I planned to string you both along for a while and see if I couldn't milk a few dollars from you both, before ditching you somewhere in the desert. But things didn't quite go to plan."

Lazarus seethed. "Vasquez, you are the biggest

cheat and scoundrel I have ever had the displeasure to know."

Mankanang stood up and all were silent as the chief began his address to his clan. He had been listening to Tohotavo all through the meal, and the pair of them had been in deep discussion as to what was to be done. His speech was a short one but spoken with the passion Lazarus had seen once before in a culture on the brink of ruin, determined to overcome the odds or go out in a blaze of glory trying. Hok'ee translated for Lazarus and Vasquez.

"Mankanang says that he will send word to the other cities. They will unite against the invaders. If the white men want a war then the people of the Seven Cities will provide one."

Chapter Twelve

In which an alliance is struck

The morning mist dissipated slowly, revealing the Confederate supply depot as if it were a ghost from another era, emerging spectrally in the secluded forest valley. Tents had been pitched over ammo dumps and machines were undergoing repair. Men in grey uniforms milled about, some on guard while others played cards and polished their weapons. They were relaxed but not so relaxed as they might have been several days ago. Even from his position behind a fallen log, Lazarus could see their twitchy hands and their casual glances to the shadows under the trees.

This was the second supply depot they had hit in three days. Reynolds had several of them set up in the southern half of the basin to reinforce his advance through the valley. Both the western and southern cities had fallen to his troops, and one of the cities in the centre of the valley would undoubtedly fall next.

Lazarus turned to the twelve Cibolans at his back. They awaited his signal, and he felt the ludicrousness of the situation; he, an Englishman who hadn't believed these people had even existed mere days ago, leading them into battle without speaking a word of their language. But he had mastered the hand signals from Hok'ee—*Pahanatuuwa*, he corrected himself—

and hoped that his signal to attack would be clear enough to them.

Vasquez and Pahanatuuwa had taken a secondary force around to the south of the depot and would form the diversion to draw the enemy's fire so that Lazarus and his squad could storm the camp and make off with its munitions. Pahanatuuwa's Jericho should provide distraction enough. The Cibolans were convinced that it was the tool to bring them victory.

The Jericho tore out three bursts of fire and the Confederates leapt up in alarm, seizing their weapons. Lazarus could feel the excitement in the Cibolans behind him and turned to make sure that none of them got carried away and charged prematurely. They held, tense and ready, as the enemy soldiers scattered in the direction of the attack. When it looked like no more would be leaving the camp, Lazarus finally gave the signal and they rushed the depot.

The remaining Confederates looked up in terrified surprise as Lazarus and his twelve Cibolans came whooping down the slope, and barely had a chance to get a shot off before they were upon them. Lazarus drew first blood, aiming his revolver at the chest of the nearest guard and hurling him backwards with a shattered ribcage. The Cibolans swung their terrible war clubs and tore through flesh with their chunks of razor-edged obsidian, splintering bone and hacking men down.

It was over in moments. Not a single Cibolan had fallen. *With more battles like this,* thought Lazarus with elation, *the Cibolans might actually stand a chance against Reynolds.* They began rooting through the supplies. The Cibolans were fascinated by the guns of the white men and seized them in great armfuls, oblivious that they required ammunition. Lazarus had considered speaking with Mankanang and Tohotavo on the matter of teaching their people how to use modern weapons. It would undoubtedly be an aid in their war, but whether or not they had time to outfit and train an army in a wholly new kind of warfare before the next battle was another matter.

They were in the process of dividing up the loot between the warriors to bear it back to their city when Vasquez and Pahanatuuwa emerged from the trees, their men at their back. "You sure let them have it," said Vasquez, looking around at the dismembered corpses.

"Well, there weren't too many of them left after your diversion," said Lazarus.

"Diversion, hell! We didn't get a shot off! They headed off in a different direction leaving us to rejoin you here!"

"What? But we heard…"

"A Jericho? So did we, but it wasn't Hok'ee's."

"Then who?"

"Search me. It came from the west and that's where the Confeds hurried off to. They went right past us. Listen! I can hear them fighting!"

Lazarus could hear it too, gunshots and cries coming from nearby. "Either they have a splinter faction in their ranks or something is sorely amiss. Could be another clan attacking them, but that was definitely a Jericho I heard."

They hurried through the trees cautiously, not wanting to blunder into whatever was happening further west. The gunfire drew nearer, and they slowed to a halt. The Cibolans, bemused as they were by this new turn of events, drew up in close formation, weapons ready. The ground sloped down from them into a rocky dip before rising up into the red mountains that formed the western wall of Cibola. It was in this dip that the fight was taking place.

"Well I'll be goddamned!" exclaimed Vasquez.

Lazarus might have said something similar had he not been lost for words. Down, in the bottom of the dip, surrounded by gun-toting figures, was the Worm. Its front portion emerged from the mountain like the head of an eel peeping out from its cave. Men and women wearing the blue of the Union stood on and around it, firing on the Confederates. At the head of the mechanical behemoth stood a woman with long blonde hair twisted into cables, holding a Springfield rifle aloft like a battle standard as she screamed for her troops to retreat.

"Townsend," said Vasquez. "And look, over there."

Lazarus saw a black man firing round after round at the advancing men.

"Thompson. So they ain't dead after all. But how in the hell did they find Cibola? We took the map with us."

Lazarus had already been scanning the fighters and had found the one he was looking for. "Katarina," he said. She was firing a Springfield rifle and picking off targets like a crack marksman, which she may very well have been for all Lazarus knew. Her dress was the same one, but torn and oily in places. Her hat was gone and her black hair hung loose. "Katarina led them here."

"She memorized the map?" asked Vasquez.

The rebels fell back behind the Worm and fired off a few answering shots as they made for the trees. The Confederates, few in number now, seemed reluctant to follow them and began to inspect the Worm; that piece of mechanical ingenuity that had eluded and frustrated their general for months.

"We'd better head back and report this to Mankanang," said Vasquez. "Although the very sight of those damned Rebs makes me wanna shoot them all right now, they may be a useful diversion and take the heat off the Seven Cities for a while."

"They may be more useful than that," said Lazarus. "What if we were to actively work together; us and Townsend's partisans against Reynolds?"

"You mean like *compañeros*?"

"Exactly."

"I ain't much for that idea. Maybe you forget, last time Townsend and I met she wasn't too friendly."

"But a common enemy can unite even the fiercest of foes."

"Well, you can explain it to Mankanang."

The chief of the northern city was about as welcoming of his plan as Vasquez had been. His people had faced annihilation at the hands of one group of white men and their guns. Welcoming a second such group as allies sounded far too dangerous. He wasn't even happy about his warriors using the captured rifles and revolvers. Already, a dire accident had been narrowly averted when one of them had fired off a round and almost hit a passing woman. Lazarus had decided to go ahead with the drilling of the men in the use of guns, with or without Mankanang's approval, if only as a safety measure.

Pahanatuuwa and his brother held counsel for a long time. It was clear that Mankanang disliked his prodigal brother but had been forced to accept him as a valuable tool against the enemy. He had already made it known that he blamed Pahanatuuwa for bringing the white men here, and if it had been up to him, he would have had him executed for clearly exile had been an ineffective punishment.

But the rest of the clan hailed Pahanatuuwa as a hero of their people. His mighty right arm and his unmatched ferocity as a warrior made up for any transgressions in their mind. It was a point of contention between the royal couple and the clan they ruled, with the latter all too happy to have these outlanders leading their warriors, and the former forced to sullenly accept them as a necessary evil.

Lazarus wasn't too sure what Pahanatuuwa had been saying to the chief, but eventually, with the urging of Tohotavo and the rest of the clan, Mankanang agreed to the plan. A large force of warriors would be assembled to rescue Captain Townsend and her troops from the Confederates and bring them back to the northern city as allies.

As the clan celebrated this new opportunity to use white man's own weapons against him, Mankanang and Xuthala seethed in their pueblo, clearly irked at having their authority trumped once more by the popularity of the returned exile.

The following day, the host assembled. Refugees had flooded in from the cities in the valley basin which was now wholly under Reynolds's control. Only the eastern and northern cities remained now. They assembled on the ridge at dawn, painted and ready for war. Lazarus itched to be off, thinking of their potential allies—and Katarina in particular—under fire. He hoped that they would get there before Reynolds had time to send reinforcements from his main army that was somewhere in the basin.

Pahanatuuwa was to lead the force with Lazarus and

Vasquez as his lieutenants at the head of flanking squads. A handful of Cibolans who looked to be the most promising sharpshooters—or at least the less likely to kill anybody on their own side—had been issued with rifles which they carried in an alarmingly casual fashion, as if they were just a different kind of war club.

Before they set out, Kokoharu came down from the pueblo to give Pahanatuuwa some parting words. And a kiss. The pair of them had grown very close over the last few days, and it pleased Lazarus to see the big fellow wear a smile once in a while. But right then, he just wished they could be off without any further hold ups. Katarina was down there, and he intended to give her a piece of his mind once they were back on the same side. He noticed Mankanang and Xuthala brooding from the doorway, surrounded by the women and children. Xuthala's scowl put her husband's to shame and seemed to deepen when Kokoharu planted a kiss on Pahanatuuwa's cheek.

The battle must have been raging all night in a series of skirmishes that had drawn the Confederates further and further from the Worm. The eyes of the Cibolans were wide as they took in this demonic behemoth from another world. It had been ransacked and detritus lay all about it; cases, tools and digging equipment.

"Check the engine room for mechanite," said Lazarus.

Vasquez and two warriors did so and returned empty handed. "Too much to hope for," the bandit said. "Reynolds won't let a single chip of the stuff fall into our hands if he can help it."

"Pahanatuuwa's supply for his gun is running low," said Lazarus. "We'll need to find some more and soon if we are to continue fighting this war."

Shots could be heard through the trees.

"You got enough mechanite for one more battle, buddy?" Vasquez called over to Pahanatuuwa.

The Cibolan nodded. He had also found a band of cartridges the Confederates had somehow missed. He slung it over his shoulder and led his men through the forest towards the sound of the fighting.

The gunfire was elusive; every time they felt they were getting close, they found that the battle had moved on to someplace else.

"We are nearing one of the central cities," said Pahanatuuwa.

The ground was rising up rapidly into a mesa that fell away in steep cliffs on all sides. It was probably the highest point in the valley; the perfect place for the Cibolans to build one of their fortresses.

"On the other side of this mesa is the lake," Pahanatuuwa continued. "The partisans have probably taken refuge in the deserted city. They would have spotted it from a distance last night."

True enough, the city was visible from the bottom of the trail that led up onto the mesa. Minarets of rock poked up out of the forest, and the houses built into them looked down on the trail like towers in a medieval castle. Springfields cracked out from one of the rock towers and they all ducked, but the shots weren't aimed at them.

"Confeds must be laying siege to the place," said Vasquez. "They can only be a little way ahead."

They pushed on through the forest and caught up with the tail end of the Confederate squad as it mounted another attack on the city.

"Come on, men!" shouted their captain. "There's

only twenty of them and nearly thirty of us! If we can wipe these rebels out, the general will give us all medals! One final push!"

Lazarus felled the man from a distance with his Springfield. The Confederates looked about in shock, knowing that it couldn't have been a lucky shot from the tower. Pahanatuuwa let his Jericho rip into them, sending them scattering. Several fell to shots from the Cibolans, and the rest fled into the city to be picked off by sharpshooters in the towers. The Confederates were trapped.

Lazarus and the rest of the attackers pursued, whooping and yelling. The Confederates sought out cover in the streets and houses of the city, and the hunt was on. Splitting up into groups, the Cibolans ducked in and out of buildings, and the sounds of gunshots and the screams of bludgeoned men echoed around the ghost town.

Vasquez called up to the towers, "Put up your guns and get down here! It's all safe now, we've come to liberate you!"

"I must say, it's not altogether too terrible to see you three," said Captain Townsend as she exited the building at the foot of one of the towers and came towards them, her uniform muddy and torn. There was blood on it too. Not hers.

"If that's the best you can do in the way of gratitude, I guess it'll have to do," said Vasquez. He still gripped his pistol.

"Relax, bandit, I'm not going to shoot you," she said.

"You'll have trouble if you do. These Cibolans here consider me a friend."

Townsend eyed the mass of painted warriors at

their backs. "Cibolans? So this is it, huh? The famous Cibola. Are you three rich as Croesus yet?" Her offhand remarks did not hide the excitement in her voice.

"Forget it," said Vasquez. "There's nothing here but peaceful natives. Reynolds hasn't got the message yet and is going through all seven cities looking for gold but finding only war."

"Seven cities? So that part is true, then?"

"That part's true, but there ain't a nugget of gold here. They got no use for it. It's all been a scam like Lazarus here has been saying all along."

"No gold..." The disappointment was barely hidden on her face.

Lieutenant Thompson snorted and muttered, "I knew it," under his breath.

Townsend glared at him. Lazarus was surprised that he was still following her orders. He was also surprised that she still kept him around after he nearly drew his gun on her back at their underground base.

"Well, that just makes everything seem like a bloody waste of time," said Katarina. Her dress was run to rags and her unkempt hair made her look wild, as did the smears of blood and mud on her cheek. She reminded Lazarus of the paintings of female French revolutionaries, leading the charge to victory, rifle in hand and banner held high.

"Katarina," he said. "It appears our respective missions are at their end. I must say, you have gone above and beyond in the pursuit of your orders. I would have thought that you would have returned home after bringing Vasquez and Pahanatuuwa into Townsend's hands."

"Vasquez and who?" The Russian replied.

"Hok'ee," Lazarus explained. "We call him Pahanatuuwa now. That's his real name. It's a long story."

"I had no choice but to remain with Captain Townsend's partisans, thanks to you. It would hardly have gone down well with my superiors had I headed home moments after you broke those two out of custody. No, I remained to see the task carried through and promised myself that I would kill you when I got the chance."

"We have a bigger enemy now," said Vasquez. "That was the whole point of us sticking our butts on the line here. The Cibolans want to offer you an alliance. Provided you don't try to loot their cities."

"If there's no gold then we have no reason to be here," said Lieutenant Thompson firmly. "We might as well return back the way we came."

"Your machine has seen better days," said Lazarus. "And Reynolds will undoubtedly send a return force to deal with you when he hears that you are in the area. We can't stay here."

"He's right," said Townsend. "The Worm will take days to fix, not to mention finding the mechanite to power her. She's grounded for the time being."

"Then you'll come back with us?" asked Lazarus. "We can organize our next move against the Confederates together."

Townsend nodded, but he could see that she was reluctant. They were trapped here. Although she hated to abandon her beloved Worm, she had no choice but to throw her lot in with the Cibolans. Her reluctance was outweighed by that of her lieutenant whom Lazarus could hear cursing under his breath as they headed away from the city.

Chapter Thirteen

In which our heroes descend into the Kingdom of the Gods

"We believed that you had all been killed by Reynolds's bombing run," Lazarus said to Katarina as they clambered up the stone steps to the northern city.

"That was a scouting patrol," Katarina replied. "I wonder, was it you who told him that we were in that area?"

Lazarus was silent.

"You bastard."

"Look, I didn't exactly tell Reynolds anything. They were spotted from the bridge of that god-awful air fortress of his."

"They were caught out in the desert chasing you. Now there's nothing left of them. Just don't mention it to Townsend. She lost a lot of good soldiers."

Lazarus glanced uneasily at Captain Townsend, but she hadn't overheard them. She was too distracted by the sight of the cliff city and its inhabitants which had turned out to meet them. But if Lazarus or any of his party had expected an ecstatic welcome praising their newest victory then they were to be disappointed for more disturbing news had reached the northern city.

The first Lazarus knew of it was the sight of even more refugees who had arrived, swelling the pueblo's population even further. Soon food would be a problem not to mention housing and sanitary conditions. The news was that these new refugees had come from the eastern city. Pahanatuuwa spoke with Tohotavo and revealed all to the outlanders.

"Reynolds has attacked the eastern city with his mortars," he said. "The entire pueblo has been leveled and most of it has slid down into the valley. There are many killed, and all surviving are now homeless. Mankanang is calling an emergency meeting."

"Poor buggers," said Lazarus as he looked around at the weeping and the wounded who had made their way along the mountain ridge. The northern city was now the only pueblo left to the Cibolans.

"Another strike against all that is decent in the world by that bastard Reynolds," said Captain Townsend. She seemed genuinely disturbed by the wailing of the children and the look of helplessness on the faces of their parents.

"We brought him here," said Lazarus. "Because of that damned map we have all been chasing."

"This wouldn't have happened if you had let me keep it!" she snapped. "But now look where you have led us!"

"I had my mission…" said Lazarus lamely.

"Damn your mission! And damn you!" She stalked off, apparently intent on helping the wounded.

"She's something of an idealist," said Katarina. "She doesn't understand people like us who aren't fighting a revolution; people who have orders instead of morals."

"Fine words from somebody who's supposed to be on her side."

"Oh, she's a good leader but her own history colors her judgment."

"How so?"

"She grew up in an orphanage. Her parents died during Sibley's invasion of New Mexico Territory. That's why she hates the Confederates more than anyone I've met."

Lazarus wondered if she hated them more than Pahanatuuwa. Everybody seemed to have their own axe to grind in this world.

Mankanang's meeting was held within the hour. The chiefs from the other cities, as well as their priests formed something of a council and all were permitted to attend. Mankanang's room was more packed than it had been when Lazarus and the others had first been brought there. After much debate, Pahanatuuwa told the outlanders what had been proposed.

"My brother is against the idea, but he has been outvoted. The other chiefs and the priests believe that the only way to defeat the enemy is to open the *sipapu*; the gateway to the kingdom of the *kachinas*."

"What on earth does that mean?" Lazarus asked. He knew that 'kachina' roughly translated to some sort of demi-god in the religion of the pueblo peoples, but this 'kingdom of the gods' was beyond his comprehension.

"Below this land lies another land wholly separate but linked to each of the Seven Cities by gateways," Pahanatuuwa explained. "It is a mirror of this world; similar, yet different. My people believe that our ancestors emerged from under the earth and so, in times of crisis, we return below ground."

Lazarus still wasn't sure what all this meant, and neither were his companions, but the Cibolans seemed to be in a state of great excitement at this news. Apparently, the kingdom of the *kachinas* was out of bounds, except on very rare occasions. He wasn't too sure how much of this underground kingdom was literal and how much was metaphorical. He noticed Mankanang arguing with Tohotavo in the corner of the room. The other chiefs got involved and Mankanang appeared to be overruled.

"What's the fuss?" he asked Pahanatuuwa.

"My brother doesn't believe that white men have any right to enter the kingdom of the *kachinas*. He thinks you should all stay here and die with your fellow invaders."

"Now that's a bit much! Haven't we fought hard enough to prove that we have no ill intentions towards your people?"

"That is what the other chiefs have argued. My brother is a vindictive man, full of spite. He doesn't even want me to be allowed to enter."

"You? But you've saved countless lives here!"

"No. I have saved some of the lives I had already put in danger."

"You're too hard on yourself."

He did not answer.

With the onset of evening, all had been prepared. Food and ammunition had been organized into bundles for the descent into the underworld, and the wounded attended to by able bodied men and women. Tohotavo led the procession into the great kiva of the pueblo. Shaped like a massive well covered with a painted mud roof, the kiva was a round subterranean room. Lazarus had read that the kiva was the ceremonial lodge or temple of the pueblo peoples, and every pueblo had several to cater to all its inhabitants. It was where the young boys slept away from their families before they reached manhood in order to be closer to the underground spirits.

A fire burned low and smoky in the dim interior and the poor light made the paintings on the walls stand out like livid, wild-eyed dancers. Lazarus focused on one that had a black face, red lips and a lolling red tongue. It was not hard to imagine a Moor visiting this valley in the time of the conquistadores and making such a name for himself that he was remembered as a *kachina*; a demi-god. *Perhaps Estevanico had been the one who had made the map after all.*

There was a circular trapdoor in the floor painted in the blacks and oranges common in pueblo art. Around this, the chiefs and their wives gathered. Ordinarily women were not permitted within the kivas, not even in a matriarchal society as that of the Cibolans. Kivas were places for the men—the decision makers of the clan—to deliberate. But this was a special ceremony that might only occur once every several generations, and the fate of them all rested upon what was about to happen.

Tohotavo began conducting his ceremony, sprinkling the ground with corn and pasting the faces of Mankanang, Xuthala and the other royal members with cornmeal. He waved feathers of turkey and eagle and shook his necklace of shell and bone. He blew his flute as the covering was pulled back from the *sipapu*; the hole-like aperture in the centre of the room that was supposedly the entrance to the subterranean kingdom.

All were silent as the black maw gaped at them. The end of an ancient looking rope ladder could be seen vanishing into the darkness below. Air, old and musty, rushed out to meet them and made the flames flicker and dance wildly. It smelled damp down there. And dead.

The chiefs were the first to enter, each taking a brand from the fire with them to light their way. It took them some time before they called up from the bottom to say that they had lit the first beacons. Then the descent of the Cibolans began.

It took an age for their turn to arrive. Women, children, priests and supplies all took precedence, and Lazarus could feel the tension in his comrades as they stood by, waiting to plunge into the unknown world. Even Captain Townsend and her rebels who had spent a good part of the last few years underground appeared a little on edge at the prospect of placing their trust in a people they didn't know. Nobody knew better than they that subterranean tunnels were dangerous places that required meticulous checks and adherence to safety regulations to prevent structural collapses.

Finally, when there was nobody else left in the kiva but the outlanders and Kokoharu, who remained as their usher into this new realm, they began their own descent. Pahanatuuwa and Kokoharu went first, then Vasquez, who grinned like a Cheshire cat at being the first non-Cibolan to set foot in the sacred kingdom of the gods. Townsend and her partisans held back, still not sure about the whole business, which just left Lazarus and Katarina.

"After you, Madam," said Lazarus.

She snorted at his chivalry and swung down the rope ladder. He clambered after her and arrived at the bottom in a pool of orange light. Pahanatuuwa and Kokoharu waited at the entrance to a long tunnel; the rest of the Cibolans having gone on ahead. They had left several sacks and bundles of supplies at the entrance for them to carry. Lazarus stood aside to let Captain Townsend down, and he allowed his eyes to linger perhaps a little too long on the shape of her backside beneath the tight material of her blue cavalry trousers. He had rarely seen women in trousers before, and the sight was surprisingly invigorating.

"Ow!" he cried as the bundle of rifles Katarina had picked up swung against his ear.

"So sorry, Longman," she said. "It's a bit cramped in here."

They headed down the tunnel which, unlike the tunnels of the Unionist Partisans, had been gouged entirely by hand. Steps were cut into the floor at occasional intervals and Lazarus wondered how many generations of Cibolans had toiled underground, building these passageways. The walls were painted with images of *kachinas* and wild angular patterns of black, white and orange.

There was a lot of light at the end of the tunnel as well as the sound of voices. The first sign that they were entering a different world was the change in texture of the walls. The murals were still present, but they were no longer painted. Instead, they had been carved out of some dark stone. The shadows were deep, and the highlights were sea-green where the light of the torches caught them.

"Turquoise…" said Vasquez, running his hands over the carven bricks that lined the passageway.

"And the floor!" cried Townsend. "It's… it's…"

They all looked down. The ground was dusty and lain with slabs of some substance softer than rock that muffled their footsteps. It had a dull sheen to it, but when a torch was held close it glimmered as if it held some potent power. Nobody said the word, as if afraid that to speak it aloud would cause all before them to dissipate in a cloud of vapor. Besides, the sight that greeted them as they exited the passageway had knocked all powers of speech from them. They had truly entered another world.

A large temple lay before them, hidden in a cavern that had been carved over hundreds of years. The ceiling was a black void above and none could see how high it was. But it was high enough to house a building the size of a museum or a large bank on Fleet Street. It rose, tier upon tier, lit from beneath by controlled fires that made every surface shimmer and gleam. Bricks the size of sheep had been laid on top of one another, made from the same substance as the floor in the tunnel.

"Gold," said Lazarus finally and the others flinched, still fearing that it might all be whipped away from them like a bad joke.

"My God," managed Vasquez. "It really does exist after all."

"It's unreal…" said Captain Townsend. "Such wealth, just sitting here beneath Arizona…"

"These temples are usually forbidden to all but our chiefs and priests," said Pahanatuuwa. "Gold is the color of the sun and is a sacred metal to my people."

"Temples?" asked Captain Townsend. "There's more than one of these?"

"Seven such as this. One for each city. One for each spiritual direction."

"Seven…" she whispered in a hoarse voice.

"You knew?" Vasquez asked his friend. "You knew the golden cities were real and you never told me?"

Pahanatuuwa replied in Navajo, and Lazarus took his reply to be along the lines of, 'So what? Would it have made a difference if I had?' He could understand that. This gold belonged to his people and none other.

The Cibolans had been making themselves at home within the temple itself, spreading out blankets, lighting fires and feeding their children. Mankanang and Xuthala had taken residence at the head of the temple, and Pahanatuuwa's brother looked even more the proud king, surrounded by his subjects within a palace of gold. They ate, and then attended an audience with the chiefs.

While the chiefs and the priests gabbled away, Lazarus let his eyes wander around the temple. He had a sudden thought. "These blocks were smelted and cast," he told Katarina. "But the North American tribes didn't have that level of metallurgy until well after this place could have been constructed."

"This valley has been isolated for so long," said Katarina. "Maybe they learned the methods independently."

"Or brought them from some other place. The Hopi have some links to the Aztecs of Mexico, particularly their language. The Aztecs smelted gold. Perhaps the Cibolans were an offshoot of that culture, much like the Hopi were, and migrated north. Only the Cibolans remembered their metallurgy whereas the Hopi forgot it."

The scholar in him was so interested in the temple itself and the culture of the people who built it that he hadn't been paying any attention to what was being discussed behind him. Pahanatuuwa was explaining the logic behind the decision to move beneath the earth.

"Each temple is connected by a series of tunnels," he said. "We can stay hidden and strike out at Reynolds from any of the Seven Cities and disappear before he can retaliate."

"It's undoubtedly an advantage," agreed Lazarus.

"But we have to be bloody careful none of the enemy gets wise to where the entrances to this underground kingdom lie. If Reynolds were to get his troops down here, these temples would quickly become tombs."

"Yes. That is why only select warriors will be chosen to go on raids. And you outlanders must remain hidden."

"Now wait just a minute, pal," said Vasquez. "I'm not going to sit down here on my rump while Reynolds cuts you fellas to pieces topside."

"Its orders from the chiefs," said Pahanatuuwa, his face apologetic. "It was a hard decision for them to allow you all down here in the first place. It has just been decided that no white man must ever leave the kingdom of the *kachinas*." He glanced at Lieutenant Thompson. "Or black for that matter."

"What!" exclaimed Captain Townsend, speaking for them all. "You can't keep us down here indefinitely! We're not your prisoners."

"No, you're not," Pahanatuuwa agreed. "You are our guests and must abide by our laws. Nobody defies the chiefs. This is done for your protection and for the protection of our civilization. They risked all by allowing outlanders to leave the valley before, and they came back in stronger numbers with weapons of unholy power. The chiefs want to end it now. The invaders must be killed and you, my friends, must never leave the valley."

"Now you just tell your damned chiefs..." began Vasquez, his face red, but Pahanatuuwa was already walking away. Kokoharu had slipped her arm around him and, with a final apologetic glance, he left them standing there gaping.

"Well, of all the..." began Vasquez. "He sure has

returned to his people, hasn't he?"

That night there was dancing by the priests to ward off the invaders. Their shadows were thrown up by the flames of the fires against the gold walls, and they leapt around causing a kaleidoscope of crazy images that made the outlanders feel like they were in a bad fever dream. The ecstasy they had experienced at finding that the myth of the golden cities was real had evaporated at the reality of their situation. They were in a gilded prison, in the very literal sense of the term. Lazarus could take no more and went for a walk around the cavern to clear his head.

He breathed the damp underground air deeply, trying to picture clear mountain views or even the fug of London to stave off his growing feeling of claustrophobia. Guards patrolled a perimeter around the edges of the cavern and scouting parties were investigating the tunnels and reporting back regularly. He followed the wall of the temple around to see how far back it went. As he passed a pillared room, he heard the voices of Captain Townsend and her lieutenant engaged in a heated discussion.

"Not long ago you were all for leaving this valley," Captain Townsend was saying. "You thought I was chasing a fairy tale, as I recall."

"That was before we found all this gold buried underground!" Thompson argued.

"So now what? You want to stay and play friendly with these people?"

"For the time being. Until we can figure out a way to ship this gold north to the Union."

"The Union..." said Townsend with bitterness. "The Union would only spend it on war machines and guns. Just a sack full of this stuff would buy up three orphanages."

"Orphanages? Does your plan for the partisan movement end there? I appreciate that you are driven by the memories of your childhood…"

"Aren't we all, Lieutenant? Don't pretend to me that you joined the partisans due to anything but your resentment at growing up on a slave plantation. The only difference between you and I is that your people were freed by an amendment to the constitution. Children still work as slaves in factories and mines paid for by the Confederate government—beaten and malnourished, choked by soot, losing fingers in machinery, living in such cramped conditions that they develop deformed spines—it's sickening, and we can end it all in Arizona Territory with just a fraction of the wealth here."

"Captain—*Theresa*—please, think for a moment. Even if we could wrestle some of this gold from these people, everything we take belongs to the Union, not to your personal liberation fund. The rest of the men have been grumbling about your leadership. They think you are losing your way."

"I am still your Captain," Townsend snarled. "And you will address me as such. I decide what is to be done with the profits our unit makes. And if you or anybody under my command insists on refusing to follow my orders, then I suggest that you all damn well stay out of my way."

Lazarus blinked in surprise. He knew Thompson wasn't a cold-hearted man, just loyal to his precious Union. Townsend was no tyrant, but her passion for her cause had turned her into a single-minded woman teetering on the brink of madness. This argument was a continuation of the one he had used to his advantage before their escape at the partisan base. Perhaps this friction between captain and lieutenant had been going on for quite some time now. That was dangerous. With enemies all around, splintering in the ranks now was something to be avoided at all costs.

Chapter Fourteen

In which a member of the party escapes

"Well perhaps you ladies and gents are content to keep your backsides in the shade," said Vasquez, "but that's my pal out there leading the advance and I ain't gonna let him take a bullet for me."

They were at the foot of the ladder that led up to the kiva in the northern city. Lazarus, Vasquez, Katarina, Thompson and a collection of partisans had accompanied the assault force that Pahanatuuwa had led down to the river. They may be forbidden from leaving the underground kingdom, but Lazarus for one wasn't going to let that stop him from aiding the Cibolans in any way he could. So, they had carried weapons for the warriors and seen them off, waiting to receive wounded on their return.

Lazarus was aware of Thompson's eyes staring at him in the dark. He knew the man didn't trust him, much less like him or any of their present company. The three men in blue uniforms at his back kept their hands on their pistols, nervous at being divided from the rest of their group. Captain Townsend had led a secondary unit through the tunnels towards the ruins of the eastern city, to hold the gateway open should the Cibolans be forced to retreat that way.

"I'm gonna go up and take a peek," said Vasquez.

He put one foot on the bottom rung of the ladder.

Kokoharu stepped forward, her dark eyes alive with warning. She had accompanied them to await the return of her beloved Pahanatuuwa and to keep the outlanders in check should they decide to defy the ruling of the chiefs.

"I appreciate your concern, doll," Vasquez said, "but we both love that big fella and if you could understand a word I'm saying, you'd know that I only have his best interests at heart."

"I don't advise it, Vasquez," said Lazarus. "She might tell the chiefs, and then what sort of bother would we be in?"

"I'm only going up to that kiva thing of theirs and taking a look-see. I won't cause no trouble and Kokoharu here is a sweet thing ain't ya? She won't tell."

He winked at her and she watched him ascend the ladder, her eyes filled with frustration. They stood back as a shower of red dust floated down in the wake of his scrabbling boots. They waited some time until they heard Vasquez call down to them; "Hey, limey! Get your ass up here!"

"That foolish bastard will have us all executed or some damn thing," said Thompson.

Lazarus ignored him and climbed up the ladder, ignoring also the voiced concerns of Kokoharu who followed him up into the kiva. Lazarus made his way over to the door where Vasquez was leaning, keeping himself in the shadows and peering through his telescope.

"Take a peek," he said, handing the brass instrument to Lazarus.

Reynolds's troops had begun the construction of a bridge over the river that sealed the northern city off from their advance. The destruction of this bridge was the object of the Cibolan attack, and through the grimy lens of the telescope Lazarus could see that they were having a rough time of it.

"It's an almighty skirmish," said Vasquez. "I wouldn't call it a battle 'cause Hok'ee ain't dumb enough to lead a full-on attack. He's hitting them hard and fast and vanishing again, but they've been quick to retaliate."

He was right. Even from their position high on the northern cliff face, Lazarus could see the Cibolan bodies littering the river. The bridge still stood, and Confederate troops were heading into the trees to flush them out. A large group of mechanicals had made its way between the Cibolans and their exit line.

"They've been cut off!" said Lazarus. As he said it, there was an enormous explosion from one of the Confederate batteries that knocked down several trees in a shower of earth.

"Holy Christ!" exclaimed Vasquez. "It's over. There's no standing up against that firepower. If they can't make it back here then they'll head towards the eastern city to Townsend and her people."

"We should head over there and help them. There's nothing to be done from here."

Kokoharu danced from one foot to the other in anxiety, knowing that something was terribly wrong but not understanding what. Lazarus took her by the arms and tried to explain that they had to make for the eastern city. He wasn't sure if he got through to her or not and had no more time to spend on the matter for soon Townsend's group would be receiving the first of the wounded.

They fled through what felt like an endless warren

of tunnels. The underground kingdom was more than just the seven golden temples connected by single passageways. There were a myriad of storerooms, dwellings, kivas and other nooks and crannies, the purpose of which was unknown to Lazarus. Kokoharu did them proud however, clearly having taken his meaning. She led the way, her fleet feet pounding down the stone floors like she was a hare fleeing the hunter.

They found the tunnels near the eastern city in a bloody nightmare of confusion. They pressed themselves against the walls as rebels and Cibolans ran past bearing wounded on woven pallets. The air was hot and dense and the close confines made the voices and screams a cacophony of ear-splitting noise.

"There's too many people here!" cried Vasquez. "These tunnels are liable to become choked up. Where the hell is Townsend?"

There were plenty of bluecoats but no sign of their leader. Pahanatuuwa squeezed passed, his right arm still smoking. Vasquez grabbed him. "Condolences, pal!" he roared in his ear. "We'll get that bridge another time. Just tell us what to do."

"Fall back to the northern temple," the Cibolan replied. "We have enough to carry the wounded and to seal the exit." His eyes searched for Kokoharu and found her already tending to a man riddled with bullets in a nearby enclave. He barked something at her and she threw him a sour glance. Evidently she wasn't prepared to give up on her patient just yet.

"Come on," said Vasquez. "We're only in the way here."

It was during the long slog back to the northern temple that Lazarus realized Thompson was no longer with them. Had they left him behind? "Where's your lieutenant?" he asked the three bluecoats who were still with them, but they just shrugged their shoulders.

They arrived barely in time to inform the Cibolans at the temple to prepare for the wounded before they started pouring in, although with nobody to translate for them it probably made little difference. There was much weeping as the news gradually sunk in that the raid had been a failure. Mankanang and Xuthala watched with grim faces as Pahanatuuwa and his remaining warriors flooded into the cavern, bearing the wounded with them.

Katarina followed Kokoharu's example and went from pallet to pallet, her sleeves rolled up, applying medical aid. Lazarus was impressed.

"Did you learn this in the Okhrana?" he asked as he helped her lift a patient from one blood-soaked stretcher to another.

She shook her head. "My uncle. He was a soldier before he joined the Interior Ministry."

"I think I may have liked him. I too was a soldier, you know? Fought in the Ashanti Campaign before I took up employment with the secret service."

"Yes, I know. And I don't think you would have liked my uncle. Nor he you."

Lazarus blinked away the hostility, gradually becoming used to it and tried to change the subject. "If only Captain Townsend and Lieutenant Thompson would show their faces; I'm sure they have some medical experience."

Katarina looked about suddenly. "They're not here? I thought they went on ahead."

"No sign of them. I heard them arguing the other night. I hope that doesn't have anything to do with it."

"Oh? Arguing about what?"

"Townsend is dead-set on using some of this gold to save children from workhouses and orphanages or some such scheme. Thompson considers it all property of the Union and won't let an ounce of it out of his sight."

"Well, it *is* the Union's property, isn't it? Or do you still harbor Confederate sympathies?"

"Certainly not. But I would have thought that the golden cities truly belong to the people who built them. The Union has no more claim to them than Reynolds."

"Nevertheless, my mission is to ensure that the Union, or at least the partisan movement, get the gold. Do you think Townsend may have deserted us and taken a quantity of gold with her?"

"It doesn't sound like her, but you know the woman better than I. All I know is that Thompson would consider that a final betrayal. He may even have pursued her with the intent of stopping her."

They finished bandaging up their patient, although it was not certain that he would live through the night. Katarina left, heading to the corner of the temple where she slept. Lazarus remained and patched up a flesh wound for a young warrior before following her in. He found her checking her ammunition and filling a canteen with water from a clay urn.

"Going somewhere?" he asked.

"Go away, Longman. I don't need you tagging along."

"You don't mean that you're going after Townsend and Thompson!"

"If both of them have deserted then I'm in a sticky spot. My superiors are relying on U.P.R. intel to ascertain that I completed my mission. They won't take my word for it alone. I need to talk some sense into them."

"Your own outfit doesn't trust you?"

She shrugged. "I could say anything I like and they have no way to check it. I need Townsend's confirmation."

"I'm coming with you."

"You'll only get in the way. Or worse, betray me to the Cibolans. They'll kill us both if they catch us trying to escape."

"You really think I'm useless, don't you? I've worked my way out of dozens of sticky situations by force and by stealth. I'm coming and you can't stop me."

"Very well." She slotted the last cartridge into her revolver and spun the cylinder. "But if I have to, I'll put you down myself, Longman."

Leaving the northern temple without being seen wasn't hard. The chiefs and priests were too busy seeing to the needs of their people and the people themselves were in too much confusion and misery to notice them slip away. The tunnels were empty and soon they were back in the chamber beneath the great kiva of the northern city.

"Are you sure they went this way?" Lazarus asked as Katarina clambered up the ladder, her skirt swishing him in the face.

"This is the closest exit," she replied. "They couldn't have escaped through the eastern city without being seen and I doubt Townsend went all the way to the western city. She had no reason to. She would have wanted to get out into the forests and hills as soon as possible. For somebody who built a tunneling machine, she really seems to hate being underground."

It was glorious to be out in the sunshine again after

so many days beneath the earth, but the heat soon got to them. They clung to the cliff walls, above the cool forests, surmising that if Townsend was trying to leave the valley, she would head south east to where the valley walls dipped down to their shallowest point. They passed the ghostly houses of the western city which were silent—like dead things with hollow eyes.

The sun began to dip below the high walls, and they welcomed the cooling touch of dusk. They stopped to rest awhile, assuming that their quarry would be doing the same, for the trek through the hills was hard going for anybody. They dared not light a fire in case they might be seen and indeed, they could see the lights of some Confederate camp or supply depot deep down in the valley.

"And so Yankee Imperialism is replaced by its Confederate cousin," Lazarus mused. "And who taught them this way of conquest? Americans have learned the art of it from us, like a child prodigy. They dream of empire themselves now; they who wanted freedom from it more than anybody. The scent of money banishes ideology from people's minds like a forgotten lover."

"You sound like the revolutionary thinkers in my own country," said Katarina, after taking a swig from her canteen. "There are some who claim that imperialism is the ultimate and unavoidable end result of capitalism."

"You do not agree with them?"

"They are dangerous traitors. Imperialism has brought light to the dark corners of the world. Roads, railways, science; the list is endless."

"I doubt the Cibolans share your appreciation of the developed world's achievements. They seemed to be doing just fine before we came blundering into their world, heralding the inevitable stamping march of empire over all that they hold dear."

Katarina looked at him for a while, her face unreadable in the darkness. "You're not quite what I expected of a British agent. What happened to you in South America? Our files are incomplete."

Lazarus took a deep breath. "I was sent there by my government. To Colombia. They had ideas to drain Lake Guatavita; the source of the Eldorado legend."

"So Eldorado really exists? Like Cibola?"

"The parallels are striking. Both were legends told to the Spaniards, who searched in vain for them despite their having a kernel of truth. Lake Guatavita lies in the Cundinamarca region of Colombia, in what was once the territory of the Muisca people. They used to have a ceremony; whenever a new Zipa—that is to say a chief—was chosen, he was floated out into the center of the lake on a raft of rushes, loaded with gold. The gold would be tossed into the lake as an offering to the goddess who dwelt there. The priests would smear the Zipa's body with some sticky substance like resin and coat him in gold dust until he was a gilded man. He would then dive into the lake and the gold would wash from his body.

"The Spaniards got the idea into their heads that if this had been going on for generations upon generations, then the bottom of Lake Guatavita must be silted in gold dust and littered with sunken treasures. They tried dredging the lake and came up with a few objects but were ultimately disappointed.

"A few years ago, a company was set up in London with the aim of draining the lake. It was funded by the government, and I was to head an advance party to explore the lake and its surroundings. The Muisca were wiped out by disease and violence soon after the Spanish conquered them, but the natives who dwell there now, although Catholic for the most part, still hold the lake in great reverence. I did not count on this and neither did my superiors.

"I found a people who, despite suffering the worst oppressions for several hundred years—or perhaps because of them—were fiercely independent. They do not even consider themselves part of the United States of Colombia, despite living within forty miles of Bogota. I fell in love with their free spirit and in love with one individual in particular.

"She was beautiful, and as strong and fiery as any of her people. As my love for her grew, so too did my disillusionment with my mission and my government's plans. What right did we have, I asked myself, to lay claim to the sacred lake of these people? The Colombian government may have endorsed our plan for their cut of the profits, but even if Lake Guatavita had been filled to the brim with enough gold to buy the world twice over, it would not have been enough for me to help my own country rob those people."

"You disobeyed orders?"

"Yes," Lazarus replied with a grim smile. "Perhaps I cannot expect a Russian agent, loyal to her Tsar, to understand, but it was during my months among the natives of Cundinamarca that I learned that some things trump fealty to one's government. I warned the girl I loved of what was coming, and she told the rest of her people. When the British arrived they found a revolt on their hands. These people were not going to let them drain their lake without a fight. And so a fight is what they got."

Katarina winced. "Natives against soldiers of the British Empire? They were wiped out?"

"Damn near every last one of them. You've seen how Reynolds has torn holes through the Cibolans. The British don't have that level of firepower, but the natives of Cundinamarca were fewer in number and less warlike. It took only a day to lay their villages to waste. The lake was soon red with their blood, and the fires of their burning homes were reflected in those dark waters."

"And the girl you loved…"

"Dead like the rest of them. I vanished then, heading north through Panama and Mexico towards the C.S.A. I had decided to wash my hands of the British Empire and their thirst for conquest."

"And yet here you are. Here *we* are."

"Yes. Here we are."

"And Lake Guatavita? Was it drained?"

"Yes. But the damned fools didn't count on the mud drying in the sun and setting like concrete. Any gold there was stuck fast and irretrievable. They abandoned the project."

Katarina watched him silently. It was cold and many hours lay between them and dawn. She moved closer to him to get some of his heat and he tried to pretend that he had not noticed. "Why did you go back into their service after that?" she asked him.

"My contact, Morton, tracked me down in some sorry shithole in the American Southwest. I was drinking myself into an early grave far from home. He persuaded me to get back up on my horse, as they say here. He had a mission for me. Something local. Find Gerard Vasquez. I may have been foolish enough or drunk enough to accept the offer then, but if I saw

Morton right now, I don't know that I wouldn't blow his brains out. He's managed to fool me into the old game of imperialism again."

"We all have our price," said Katarina.

"What was yours?"

"That's a long story."

"It's a night for telling stories. Where in Russia are you from?"

"Smolensk. My father was an impoverished nobleman. When he died my mother sent me to live with my uncle."

"The one in the Okhrana?"

"There's really no such thing, you know? That is a word the enemies of the Tsar thought up to cover all of the different clandestine agencies of the Internal Ministry. But yes, my uncle is a high-ranking member. He raised me. I'd rather not go into it all now, if that's all the same with you."

"All right. You must of course feel free to remain the woman of mystery for me."

"You're one to talk. I don't know a thing about you. I mean, I've read your file but I know nothing about your childhood."

"You never asked."

"There's hardly been time in between getting shot at. Very well. Tell me about your parents."

"Don't remember them. They died when I was very young. I was adopted by a learned man who raised me as his own."

"And so you were saved from the notorious workhouses of London. How Dickensian."

"Actually I was saved from something altogether different. And I'm not from London."

"Oh?"

"That's all I want to go into right now."

"Come on, where were you born?"

"When you feel like telling me more about your uncle and your childhood, then I'll tell you about how that kind gentleman found me on the streets of a foreign city and took me into his care."

"Very well. Perhaps if we live for a few more days." She was quiet for a moment. "I don't know why, Longman, but I hate you more than I've hated any man I've ever known."

Lazarus felt that accepting this latest insult seemed a fair price to pay for the liberty of putting his arm around her. She rested her head on his shoulders and they said no more.

Chapter Fifteen

In which blood is spilt between comrades

They moved at first light. It promised to be a hot day and they were keen to find water before they ran out entirely. The river cut close to the foot of the cliffs, and they descended to drink and refill their canteens. A gunshot sounded nearby, and they flung themselves flat, drawing their weapons. Katarina belly-crawled towards a boulder and pressed her back to it, peering into the trees up ahead.

Lazarus rose, confident that the shot had not been aimed at them. His Starblazer held steady, he entered the shade of the trees. Katarina followed close.

"Are you two going to just stand there?" came a voice from above them.

They looked up and saw Lieutenant Thompson perched in the branches of a ponderosa, his blue uniform dusty and torn. One leg hung down on either side of a branch. The left was dark to the knee with blood.

It was only then that Lazarus saw the mountain lion. Its beige fur camouflaged it against the dusty rocks and bronze pine needle carpet. But nothing camouflaged its snarl. Lazarus and Katarina took quick, involuntary steps backwards.

"Shoot it, for Chrissake!" yelled Thompson.

Lazarus aimed his revolver at the face of the beast and looked it dead in those honeyed eyes. His finger squeezed the trigger, but the lion turned tail and loped off, the roar of the Starblazer spurring its retreat until it vanished into the trees.

Lazarus didn't know how long Thompson had been up in that tree. Perhaps all night, but he certainly seemed eager to get down from it. They helped him plant his feet back on solid ground, although he limped terribly.

"Let me look at that leg," said Katarina.

"Damned cat caught me just before I got out of its reach," said Thompson, wincing as he sat down. "It's been circling my ass for hours."

"Can't cats climb trees?" asked Lazarus.

"You bet. He's a nimble bastard, but the noise of my gun kept him from scrambling up here. Only got five cartridges left."

"We heard you spend one. Lucky for you we were passing by."

Thompson screwed his face up as Katarina tightened the torn strip of her dress that she was using as a bandage around his calf. "Yeah, what are you two doing snooping around here anyway? Didn't those underground lunatics try and stop you leaving?"

"They didn't stop you, did they?" said Katarina. "You're welcome by the way."

"We got wind that your captain left us," said Lazarus. "And you after her. What's it all about?"

Thompson narrowed his eyes. "I don't usually discuss partisan affairs with strangers. Especially not those working for the C.S.A."

"I don't work for them anymore. I would have thought that the last few days would have proved that."

"Well, Townsend's just gone crazy, I figure," he replied. "She took off when we were holding the entrance to the northern temple. Desertion is what it is. I never thought it of her, but she's been acting pretty strange in recent months. Obsessed with things that have nothing to do with our mission. She's lost her mind and taken off with no regard for the troops she's left behind. That's just plain treachery in my book. I'd have hung her if I were her superior."

"But you aren't," said Lazarus. "So what are you going to do?"

"I tell you what *I'm* going to do," said Katarina. "I'm going to beat the living hell out of her for ditching me in this valley. Does she think I'm here for the mountain air? I have a mission and she's near ruined it for me."

"Join the queue," said Thompson as he staggered to his feet and began testing the strength in his leg. The bandage held but was already spotted with seeping blood.

"You'll need stitches," said Katarina. "I'll see what I can do back at base camp, but that should hold for now."

"She hasn't got more than a couple of hours on us if she stopped to rest," said Thompson. "If we hurry, we'd catch up with her, it's just my leg…"

"Just try and keep up with me," said Katarina. "Longman, you help him."

"Get your hands off me," snapped Thompson as Lazarus tried to offer his support. "I can hobble along well enough on my own."

Hobble he did but admirably, matching Lazarus and Katarina pace for pace as they rose up out of the forest and continued following the cliffs to the southern point, where they dipped down. He was clearly struggling, and the strip of Katarina's dress wasn't enough to keep the blood in his body.

It was a brutal trek. Before the sun had reached its zenith, they had caught up with the lone figure of Captain Townsend whom they saw wandering through the shimmering heat waves like a ghost. She was weighed down by a knapsack that looked like it was bursting at the seams and the weight of it made her stagger.

"Captain!" called out Thompson.

She whirled in surprise. Thompson drew his pistol and aimed it at her. Townsend returned the favor. Katarina drew her own and aimed it at Thompson.

"Let's just be calm..." said Lazarus, his hand hovering near his own pistol, unsure that if he drew it, who he would point it at.

"Go back, Lieutenant!" called up Townsend. "That's an order."

"Order?" scoffed Thompson. "I don't take orders from deserters. Townsend, I am escorting you back to camp and relieving you of command!"

"I'm warning you, Thompson..."

"As am I," said Katarina. "You shoot her and I'll put a bullet in you before she hits the ground."

Thompson ignored her and descended the slope, keeping his gun on his captain. Katarina followed close. "What's in the knapsack?" he asked her.

She didn't answer but un-looped one strap and dropped it to the ground. It landed with a dull thud. Its seams split and its contents slid out. Gold glinted in the sun; enough gold to buy several large farms.

"Goddamn you, Townsend..." said Thompson. "You're nothing but a lousy traitor out for your own profit."

"You think this gold is for me?" she snapped back. "You think I give a damn about bits of metal? This gold can pay for some of the blood this war has drained from my homeland. It can buy up an orphanage or two. It can reimburse some families who have lost everything."

"And what of the partisan rangers?" asked Thompson. "And the Union? They need this gold too."

"Damn the Union! I haven't fought my way out of the gutter and lost countless friends here in Arizona to hand everything over to them!"

Thompson had set his face to that of a cold statue. Lazarus saw his gun arm tense.

"Thompson, no!"

The gun roared and Townsend fell backwards, her own gun remaining unspoken, Thompson's bullet lodged somewhere deep within her. She staggered and then her legs gave out and she fell, her unbound lion's mane of twisted hair spreading out around her head like a halo of gold.

Thompson ignored the barrel of Katarina's gun that was only a few inches from his temple. If she was going to shoot him then she would have done it already. He holstered his pistol.

"I should kill you right now," she hissed.

"And that would achieve precisely what?" Thompson replied. "You were too slow to save her and now it's done." He bent down and began scooping the gold back into the knapsack.

"Why couldn't you have just let her go?" Lazarus asked him.

He glared at him under his heavy brow. "She was a traitor and a deserter. This is how it is in the army.

Besides, she nearly drew on me."

"Her reasons did not seem wholly selfish. What is a sack full of gold when there are seven cities of the stuff here?"

"It is not the amount that counts but the intention. This gold belongs to the Union. Townsend lost her faith in the Union, I don't know when, perhaps long ago. I had my suspicions but should have acted sooner. There's no helping such as her." He rose and looked at Katarina. "I am now in command of the Arizona Territory Unionist Partisan Rangers. I shall pass on my good words to your superiors. Townsend's death will not affect your mission."

Katarina spun and strode away.

"You're a cold man, Thompson," said Lazarus.

"Who isn't in this world?"

They made their way back north, Thompson hobbling to keep up with Katarina's furious pace, the gold abandoned. When they came within sight of the western city something made her halt and step into the shade of the pines.

"What is it?" Lazarus asked.

She pointed up at the deserted pueblo. It did not seem so deserted now. Figures were moving about between the buildings. Figures in uniforms.

"What are they doing back here?" Lazarus asked. "There's surely nothing of interest left in those hovels."

"Stay out of sight," said Katarina. "Last thing we need is to be spotted by them now."

Thompson's eyes glared up at the Confederates, his hand brushing his revolver. He clearly wished he had firepower and opportunity enough to take them all on. They trod the soft floor of the forest in perfect silence, or at least they assumed so. Somebody had heard them. A figure rose up sharply from the foliage causing all three of them to draw their guns.

"Don't shoot her!" hissed Lazarus.

It was Kokoharu. She looked surprised to see them but not, Lazarus was willing to wager, as surprised as they looked to see her. Her keen ears had most certainly picked up their approach.

"What on earth are you doing out here?" Lazarus asked her, forgetting for the moment that she could not understand English. "Don't you know that a party of the enemy is up at your old city?"

The jerk of his head in that direction elicited a fierce response from the girl and she began to gesticulate, showing that yes, she knew very well that the enemy had returned to the home of her clan. From the ensuing monologue, Lazarus could pick out only the names of people he knew; Mankanang and Xuthala were mentioned, as was Pahanatuuwa along with some variant on the pronunciation of Vasquez's name. She kept pointing up at the cliffs.

"They're all up there?" asked Lazarus. "Vasquez and Pahanatuuwa? And Mankanang and Xuthala? Up at the city?"

She nodded.

"What the devil has been going on?" he demanded, but Kokoharu had turned and was making her way through the foliage, leaving the outlanders with no choice but to follow.

"Do you suppose they've been captured?" Katarina asked Lazarus.

"Unlikely. The chief and his wife, along with their greatest warrior, and Vasquez who shouldn't even be out in daylight? That's too lucky for Reynolds. I'm guessing Mankanang and Xuthala are discussing terms with Reynolds. They probably brought Pahanatuuwa along as an interpreter. And Vasquez? Who knows? Something to do with his relationship with Reynolds is my guess. All the same this is very fishy."

Kokoharu led them to a little squashed area in the bushes where some brush had been piled up to form a soft bed. Here she picked up her spear.

"Poor lovesick child has been sleeping here all night," said Lazarus. "Must have followed them and kept a watch over Pahanatuuwa to see that he would come to no harm."

"What's she doing now?" Katarina asked.

Kokoharu was setting off towards the cliffs, spear in hand, as if she was going to singlehandedly conquer the Confederate army.

"I think our presence has made up her mind to attack," Lazarus replied.

Kokoharu stopped suddenly and impatiently beckoned them to follow. Lazarus drew his pistol.

"You're not thinking of following this insane creature up to the city?" Thompson exclaimed.

"I'm not asking you to come with me, either of you," said Lazarus. "But my friends are up there, and I do not leave friends in such perilous straits. And also, it may be worth remembering, Thompson, that there are plenty of Confederates up there that require killing."

Thompson said nothing but drew his revolver and looked at it as if in longing. Lazarus reached into his pocket, drew out a couple of boxes of Colt cartridges and tossed them to him.

Chapter Sixteen

Another betrayal

"I don't trust that bastard with a loaded gun," said Katarina.

"Neither do I, but I reckon he will be more concerned with shooting at the enemy than at us for the present," said Lazarus. "A loose cannon can be a powerful weapon so long as one is willing to take a gamble."

"I didn't think you were a gambling man," muttered Katarina.

"Let's proceed carefully, at all costs," said Lazarus as they scrambled up the slope on the left side of the city. "If there are any negotiations going on, I would hate to spoil them and bring our comrades close to peril."

Kokoharu, as if anticipating this, led them on a round-a-bout trail that concealed them from the sight of any guards in the city. They soon found themselves on a ridge high above the flat rooftops. Lazarus caught the whiff of boiling coffee from somewhere below, and his body ached for such comforts which had been denied him since their arrival in Cibola. Several guards patrolled the rooftops with Whitworth sniper rifles.

"Are you any good with those at a distance?" Lazarus asked Thompson. "I'm a fair shot myself but it's your leg I'm thinking of."

"Leave it to me," the lieutenant replied. "I'll pick the bastards off one by one while you two go in and do what you have to do on the ground."

"Capital idea. Katarina? Are you ready?"

She cocked her pistol by way of reply. Kokoharu lay down her spear and drew a wicked-looking obsidian knife from her belt before dropping down onto the nearest roof.

They followed her as silently as they could, desperately wishing that they were as stealthy as the nimble-footed Cibolan. Hopping from one roof to another, ensuring that nobody on the adjacent roofs could see them, they made their way towards the nearest sniper.

Lazarus made the kill. Creeping up on the guard from behind, he grabbed him in a lock and slipped his bowie knife out and up to his throat, drawing it hard and fast across esophagus, jugular and vocal cords. The man went down with a barely audible choking and coughing as blood filled his lungs and he asphyxiated. Lazarus plucked up the Whitworth and tossed it to Thompson.

With the partisan covering them from the roof, Lazarus, Katarina and Kokoharu slipped down to street level and made for the shadows of the next building. Ordinarily, Lazarus would have balked at the idea of leading two young women into a danger zone, but he had fast learned that Katarina could take care of herself, and Kokoharu seemed as determined to rescue his friends as he did. Besides, everything he had seen of her so far suggested that she might be a lethal killer when she had a mind to be.

A shot rang out behind them. They looked up and saw a Confederate fall backwards on the roof ahead of them. Thompson was a fine shot indeed, but all cause for stealth now was gone. The battle had begun.

Two Confederates came running around the corner and Lazarus blasted them both, low and fast while Katarina sent a third tumbling back through the doorway he had emerged from across the street. Lazarus lamented the spilled coffee pot as they hurried past, seeking cover as Thompson fired two more shots above their heads. There couldn't be many more guards left on the rooftops. In fact, the whole pueblo had gone very silent.

"They must be hiding somewhere indoors," said Lazarus.

As he finished speaking, a burst of Jericho fire illuminated the doorway to the kiva up ahead. Lazarus figured they would have a mechanical or two. It came lumbering out of the round building, firing as it advanced. They ducked down behind a low wall, drawing its fire. Bullets ate into the brick, rapidly reducing it to dust, its soft construction no match for the 45-70 rounds. The magazine ran empty and Lazarus poked his head up over the ruined wall, hoping to get a lucky shot in before the mechanical finished reloading.

Before he could fire, a small, lithe figure leapt onto the mechanical's back and wrapped her legs around its middle. Lazarus hadn't even noticed Kokoharu leave them, but she had clearly found a sneaky way around the buildings and was now plunging her obsidian knife between the head and right shoulder of the behemoth again and again, causing the blood of the pilot to run out across the hot metal. It sagged to its knees and slumped forward. Kokoharu slid off the bronzed carcass and held her bloodied fist that gripped the blade aloft like a hunter reveling in victory after bringing down a stag.

Lazarus and Katarina whooped and cheered, but the little Cibolan was smart enough not to loiter near the doorway to the kiva. She rolled away just as two shots whistled out of the dark opening.

"They're holed up inside," said Lazarus, thumbing new cartridges into his Starblazer. "We've got them cornered."

"But how to get them out?" said Katarina. "And how to stop them retreating further? You know what lies in the floor of every kiva."

Thompson had descended from his rooftop vigil and joined them. Single file, with Lazarus carefully leading, they approached the kiva. Peering in, Lazarus could see that the Confederates had descended the ladder to the room below. They entered the building and stood around the hole in the ground. Thompson held out his rifle and called down.

"I give up! I'm wounded and give you my weapon!" He let the rifle drop and they heard it clatter on the floor below. There was movement. Voices. Somebody picked up the rifle.

They'll never fall for this, thought Lazarus.

But to his surprise, somebody was coming up the ladder. Lazarus let the soldier put his hands on the top rung and poke his head up before kicking savagely with his boot and sending the dazed Confederate tumbling back down into the kiva. Lazarus jumped after him and landed on his body.

There were four more men in the room. Lazarus had noted them and started to fire before they even knew they had an invader in their midst. He fanned his Starblazer as Vasquez would do, sending all six bullets at belly height around the room and into their intended targets. The noise was deafening within the subterranean room, and the blaze of each round lit the confined space up like an electrical storm. Men fell, clutching their guts and chests.

"Damn me, limey!" hooted Vasquez from somewhere unseen. "We'll make a frontier gunman of you yet!"

They were tied together on the floor in the corner of the room, the ropes digging into Pahanatuuwa's thick biceps. Lazarus drew his knife and cut them loose.

"What's the devil's been going on here?" he asked them. "We believed you both to be captured or drawn in on some hair-brained scheme to talk terms with Reynolds."

"First one, then the other," said Vasquez, climbing to his feet and rubbing some life back into his limbs. His face was bloody and swollen, as was Pahanatuuwa's, suggesting some rough treatment at the hands of their captors. "After the failure to destroy the bridge, Mankanang lost all hope and concocted a scheme to offer Reynolds one of the Seven Cities in exchange for peace. He was going to hand it over to him without the other chieftains knowing!"

"He's mad if he thinks that would satisfy Reynolds. One golden city will never be enough for him, or the C.S.A. for that matter."

"But Mankanang and Xuthala don't know Reynolds as we do. They roped us along on the pretense of being their translators, but we knew nothing of their plan to surrender the western temple. Turned out we were to be a sweetener on the deal. They were going to hand us over to Reynolds as compensation for the lives lost in the recent skirmishes."

"Where are they now?"

Vasquez nodded to the doorway that led to the tunnels. "Showing Reynolds around his new golden palace. But what happened to you and Katarina? Nobody's seen hide nor hair of you since the battle."

"On the trail of Townsend," answered Lazarus.

"Whatever happened to that hussy anyway?"

"Dead. She tried to make a run for it with a sack of stolen gold. Thompson killed her."

Vasquez eyed the partisan. "You don't say. Wouldn't have thought it of her, but you never can tell, as they say."

At the sight of Kokoharu, Pahanatuuwa's eyes grew wide and angry and he began to shout at her in Cibolan. Lazarus intervened on her behalf.

"She was waiting outside the city for you, Pahanatuuwa. Like a guardian angel. It was she who led us in. And you're not the only Cibolan who can claim to have felled a mechanical now."

The big warrior's eyes softened, and he looked down at Kokoharu's bloody right hand. A faint smile of pride touched his lips.

Vasquez whistled. "What a crew. Now I don't know about you fellas, but I'm dying to put an end to this whole silly business and pay back Reynolds for all he's done. You all with me?"

"I couldn't have put it better myself," said Lazarus.

"My brother and his wife must also pay for their treachery," said Pahanatuuwa. "With their lives, preferably." And he was the first to return to the kingdom of the *kachinas*.

The western temple was similar to its northern counterpart but built in a slightly different way. It still rose tier on tier much like the pueblo above it, slabs of gold studded with turquoise that glimmered softly by the light of the torches.

Before they had got within two steps of the cavern, a sniper shot rang out and showered them with flakes of rock. They dived for cover, Vasquez firing in the general direction of the temple. The sniper could be seen reloading on a golden terrace three floors up. Thompson knelt, rested his Whitworth on a boulder, aimed and fired. The sniper fell back with a cry.

"Come on!" cried Vasquez. "In and at them!"

They hurried up the golden steps and spilled into the temple. There was no sign of Reynolds or the Cibolan traitors in the great room.

"They must be in one of the side rooms or upstairs," said Lazarus. "Fan out but stay in pairs."

Vasquez and Pahanatuuwa headed towards the storerooms on the far side of the temple while Lazarus and Katarina made for the stairs at the rear of the audience chamber. Thompson and Kokoharu remained and took up position in the great room should their quarry return that way.

The chambers above were deathly silent. Lazarus knew that there must be more guards on the upper levels, so they proceeded cautiously, checking each corner of every room. They passed the bloodied corpse of the sniper Thompson had slain; laying on his back, a pool of blood slowly expanding across the gold slabs. They heard shots below and knew that Vasquez and Pahanatuuwa had come across some more Confederates.

As they entered a large, unlit room on the uppermost floor of the temple, Lazarus heard the click of a revolver being cocked. The metal walls caused the sound to echo. He had just enough time to duck as the pistol fired and sent its bullet thudding into the soft gold walls. By the light of the blazing round, Lazarus had seen the face of General Reynolds and several of his soldiers, limed in orange like demons from hell.

"Back out of here!" Lazarus cried as Katarina sent three bullets towards Reynolds to no effect.

Once outside the room, they stood on either side of the door, their weapons ready.

"There must be another entrance," Katarina whispered so Reynolds could not hear her plan. "Every room in these places has at least two, or so it seems."

"Agreed," Lazarus whispered back. "You stay here, and I'll go around. Maybe I can come in on them from a side door."

He hurried along the terrace and around the corner, searching for the door. A massive figure with copper skin and long black hair charged out of a doorway on the other side and barreled into him. At first Lazarus thought it was Pahanatuuwa, but the fierce determination of the man to disarm him made him realize that this was Mankanang.

His Starblazer slid across the gold flags, knocked from his grasp as he went down under the big Cibolan. He found himself powerless as the giant wrenched him to his feet and hauled him back in through the doorway from which he had come. He was shoved without ceremony to the feet of the beautiful Xuthala.

She smiled at him in her cold triumph. He tried to rise to his feet, but she seized him, spun him around and pressed an obsidian blade with a wicked edge against his jugular. She barked something at her husband, and several figures hurried past the doorway. Lazarus wanted to cry out, for he saw Vasquez and

Pahanatuuwa, but the blade digging into his neck made any such movement extremely difficult.

Xuthala marched him out onto the terrace. His English spirit was utterly humiliated at being treated in this way by a woman, but the strength in her lithe, coppery arms and the quickness of her blade banished any foolish thoughts of bravado. Up ahead, Vasquez and Pahanatuuwa had joined Katarina at the doorway to the room that held Reynolds.

Mankanang bellowed something which made his brother spin around. The two parties stared at each other for a while, each willing the other to make the first move. Naturally, it was Vasquez who took the initiative.

"Well, your brother's got us by the nuts, pal," he said to Pahanatuuwa. "Much as that limey has been a pain in the ass, I've grown a little fond of him. I can't let that hellcat ruin his shirt with his own blood. What's next?"

Pahanatuuwa and his brother held a quick counsel.

"They want us to let Reynolds go," Pahanatuuwa said. "You are to go with him. They say that white men can have the western temple but must not defile the kingdom of the *kachinas* further with their hostilities. You are to take your differences to the world above."

"And what of you?" Lazarus said, risking the bobbing of his Adam's apple against Xuthala's blade.

"I am to remain here and face the judgment of my brother's counsel."

"Hear that, Reynolds?" Katarina shouted into the room. "You're free to go."

"Now wait a minute," said Vasquez. "We can't leave Hok'ee here to answer to all we've done. And it churns my guts to see that bastard Reynolds walk away just when we had him."

From a doorway further down the terrace they saw General Reynolds and his three remaining soldiers step out. Reynolds called out, "I'd surely love to catch up and reminisce, Vasquez. Perhaps there'll be time for that topside!"

Pahanatuuwa's eyes bulged at the sight of his sworn enemy vanishing down the stairs. To have come so close to his revenge and yet be forced to let it slip through his fingers must have been a terrible strain on his sense of honor. The strain became too much and he let out a primal roar as he lunged forward towards Lazarus and Xuthala.

Lazarus thought his number was up as the giant slammed into them. He felt Xuthala's blade graze his neck and the warm blood run down. He did his best to get out of the mess as Pahanatuuwa's big hands grasped Xuthala around the neck. She tried to cry out but was cut off as his fingers pressed in deep, choking her.

Mankanang bellowed some challenge and made for his own brother, but Vasquez was ready and brought up his revolver. He sunk two bullets into the chief, and then a third as the enraged Cibolan reared up and turned on him. The fourth went between his eyes and the brute fell backwards without a sound, landing heavily on the terrace.

Pahanatuuwa let out a cry of anguish, not for his brother, but for the woman he finally let slip from his grasp. Xuthala was dead, her eyes white and wide, her neck crushed.

"Didn't think he'd ever turn on her, no matter what she did," Vasquez said.

Lazarus rubbed at the blood on his neck. "What do

you mean?"

"Remember the woman I told you he was exiled over? The one who ditched him for another man?"

"Yes."

Vasquez indicated the corpse of the woman who lay beneath the grieving form of Pahanatuuwa. "You're looking at her."

"And Mankanang…"

"Was the other fella. His own brother. What a deuce. They sure deserved each other."

They heard shots down below and figured that Reynolds had run into Thompson and Kokoharu. They hurried down the stairs and found one dead Confederate and Thompson holding a smoking rifle while looking longingly at the doorway to the temple.

"I aimed for Reynolds but hit one of his troopers instead," he told them. "Damn it! They went back up the tunnels to the city."

"Reynolds will be back," said Lazarus. "And with his whole army now that he knows the way down here. We should get back to the northern temple and warn them."

Kokoharu looked at Pahanatuuwa. She sensed the great sorrow in his heart and went to embrace him. He grasped her and held her close, but his fierce spirit refused to let any tears escape.

Chapter Seventeen

The Cataclysm

The news that the chief of the northern clan and his wife were dead was met more with shock than mourning back at the northern temple. And the news that the enemy now knew the way down into the kingdom of the *kachinas* set everybody trembling with fear. Tohotavo and the other priests held a council within the temple. The chiefs were called in, and Pahanatuuwa too, which surprised everybody, not least himself. Once the meeting was adjourned, Pahanatuuwa rejoined Lazarus, Vasquez and Katarina, who were sitting on the steps outside.

"The council has decided on a drastic maneuver," he told them. "If the enemy comes down here in strong numbers, which I believe they will, then we are to abandon the kingdom of the *kachinas* and return to the world above."

"You're just going to let them have the golden cities?" Lazarus asked.

He shrugged his massive shoulders. "It makes more sense than all of us dying down here. If Reynolds is so desperate for the golden cities then he can have them. Forever."

"What do you mean?"

"How much explosives do we have?" he asked Vasquez.

"Plenty after the partisans joined us," the bandit replied. "They had a load aboard that Worm of theirs. Why?"

"I have explained the power of dynamite to the council. They are keen to see it put to use against the enemy."

"Wait a minute," Lazarus said. "If we start tossing dynamite around down here, we're liable to have the ceiling down on our heads."

"That's the idea," said Pahanatuuwa.

They stared at him, sure that something had been misunderstood. "Come again?" said Vasquez.

"Right above our heads lies the lake," explained Pahanatuuwa. "If we blow away certain strategic points, we can bring the whole thing down, flooding the tunnels and concealing the golden cities forever. Naturally we will have made our way back to the surface before this happens, leaving Reynolds and his army to perish down here. All would be buried beneath the lake."

"You can't do that!" said Katarina. "To render such wealth forever irretrievable is madness!"

Pahanatuuwa glared at her. "The decision is for the council to make. You are all guests here."

She knew he was right, but Lazarus could sympathize with her outrage at the idea. Unlike him, she still retained some hope of completing her mission, despite the death of Townsend. How could she return to her homeland having taken part in the ruination of the plan to finance the Union?

The remaining partisans were even more outraged than Katarina was once the plan was outlined to their new captain. "Surely there must be another way," said Thompson. "We can't just abandon the golden cities!"

"You heard the man," said Vasquez, referring to Pahanatuuwa. "It's not up to us. If the council says it is to happen then that's what will happen."

"This is ludicrous!" Thompson could be heard muttering as he went to rejoin his troops.

That evening Lazarus and Vasquez drew up a plan of the subterranean kingdom on the lid of a wooden crate, using a stick blackened in the fire. Pahanatuuwa and Tohotavo told them of the weak points in the supports that, if blown, would bring down the lake. They also made some calculations, then set aside an amount of dynamite and enough fuse to give them plenty of time to escape.

"So," said Vasquez, biting the end off a cheroot and jamming it in his mouth. "Who is joining this crazy party while all the sane people here get their hides topside?"

Lazarus snatched the match from his fingers before he lit the cheroot, seated as he was, atop a crate of dynamite. "You, me, and Pahanatuuwa," he said. "Tohotavo's knowledge of the kingdom would be invaluable, but I fear his years would not allow him to keep up. It will be a fast run out of here once the fuses are lit."

"Sure, sure," said Vasquez, finding a safer spot to sit before fumbling for another match. "What about the Russkie?"

Lazarus looked over towards Katarina, who was helping Kokoharu in the organization of the people for yet another upheaval. "I fear that her views on our plan make her a liability. Thompson also. We're going at this without them, just the three of us."

"Fine by me."

They ate a hearty meal of broth, corn and flatbread,

which had been set aside for them from the supplies that had already been packed and sent on up to the northern city. The exodus of people had begun to move too, leaving the golden temple which for days had rung with the sound of a civilization eerily quiet, as it must have stood for generations before. Tohotavo and two of his fellow medicine men remained to bless the three *compañeros* who were about to embark on their mission of madness. They endured the traditional warrior ceremony of the Cibolans; marked with iron manganese and dusted with corn flour while Tohotavo shook his fetish stick to the beating of the rawhide drum.

Once the priests had departed, Lazarus looked at his companions. Pahanatuuwa looked every inch the ferocious Cibolan warrior apart from his metal arm, to which he had affixed a Golgotha rifle, but Vasquez looked like a bizarre clown from somebody's nightmare, with a pasty face and black shadows smeared around his eyes. Lazarus imagined that he looked somewhat similar and hoped that they would at least put some fear into their enemy should they come across them in the tunnels.

They set off, carrying the dynamite and fuse upon a primitive cart. Pahanatuuwa led the way with his torch held a safe distance away from the cart, while Lazarus and Vasquez pushed it along, cursing the shoddy wooden wheels and feeling the darkness closing in behind them like a shroud as they went deeper and deeper under the lake.

All passageways met at the center of the underground kingdom like the middle point of a gigantic cobweb. They moved in a clockwise direction, wiring the dynamite to the wooden supports pointed out on their crude map, trailing the fuse along the passageways as they went. They worked through the night, wiring up the passageways that led to the eastern and southern temples. As they neared the western temple, Lazarus halted in his wiring and strained his ears.

"What is it?" Vasquez asked.

"I can hear voices up ahead."

They went silent and listened. There was indeed the sound of voices coming down the passageway towards them.

"Reynolds," said Vasquez.

"Quick!" said Lazarus. "Unwire this lot. Hide the fuse. They mustn't see what we are doing."

They stuffed the bundle of dynamite back into the cart and kicked dust over the end of the fuse before hauling their load into one of the nearby storerooms. They had just got the cart and themselves out of sight, when the light of a torch appeared around the corner.

"How long do these damned passageways go on for, General?" asked a drawling southern voice. "I don't much like creeping about like moles. What if the entrance should collapse and we all get stuck down here?"

"Can it, Major," said the unmistakable voice of Reynolds. "Those savages manage to live down here without bother. What's the matter with you? Didn't you see that temple? There's seven of those things down here. Enough gold to win the war ten times over and make gentlemen of us all into the bargain. Quit your bellyaching and keep up."

"I been thinking about these temples, General," continued the Major. "How are you planning to get the gold topside?"

"We'll build a winch and derrick system and shift it brick by brick."

"And ship it out in dirigibles?"

"Too slow. The dirigibles can't carry all that much gold in a single flight. We'll finish that railway through the mountains that the Yankees built with that subterranean doohickey of theirs. Most of the work's been done for us already."

Lazarus, Vasquez and Pahanatuuwa held their breaths as the company passed by. Once they were gone, Vasquez drew his revolver. "Let me pop him right in the back of the head!"

"No!" hissed Lazarus, grabbing his hand. "We've still got work to do and we don't want half their army coming down here. I only hope they don't spot any of the dynamite we've already rigged up."

They dragged the stubborn cart back out into the passageway and continued with their mission. Having wired the points furthest west, they abandoned the cart in a storeroom and headed north, hoping that they would not stumble onto the heels of Reynolds's party.

"They may have discovered the northern temple by now," said Vasquez. "How are we planning to bypass them and make our exit?"

"The eastern city is too risky after the battle," said Lazarus. "It's a good bet a large part of the Confederate army is loitering around there. We could head down to one of the cities in the valley and walk back north on the surface."

"As long as it isn't that island city. I ain't much of a swimmer."

Any further discussion on the matter was cut short as footsteps could be heard approaching. They looked around frantically, seeing no handy storeroom they could duck into this time. Hopelessly cornered, they drew their weapons and prepared for the worst.

They had the element of surprise on the Confederates who rounded the corner, and opened fire before their enemy could even draw their weapons. The tunnel was filled with shouts and deafening roars of pistols and the *boom-boom!* of Pahanatuuwa's Golgotha. Several gray shirts fell dead and, in the flashes, Lazarus saw the black face of Thompson, his eyes livid with terror.

Two Confederates were left alive, and they stumbled over the corpses of their comrades, firing as they retreated. They had left their prisoner behind them, squirming in the dust. His hands were bound behind his back.

"Thompson!" exclaimed Vasquez. "What the hell are you doing here?"

"Came to join you," the partisan replied. "But Reynolds's men captured me. Will one of you please untie me?"

Vasquez released him and helped him to his feet but eyed him suspiciously.

"Where were they taking you, Thompson?" Lazarus asked.

"West temple, I figure."

"So, the north temple is taken?"

"As good as having the bars 'n' stars flying from its tip. Reynolds is on his way there."

"We almost ran into him. And why the sudden change of heart? You made your opinion of our plan plain enough earlier."

Thompson shrugged. "Couldn't leave you three to die at the hands of my enemies. Besides, I came within a hair's breadth of killing Reynolds before and I don't want to miss that chance again."

Something didn't feel at all right about Thompson's story, but they had no time to argue. The tunnels beneath the northern half of the lake were clearly infested with Confederates. They quickly referred to their map and made for the tunnels that led to the central cities. But the two Confederates who had got away had returned with reinforcements and were in hot pursuit.

They reached a junction in the tunnel complex and were momentarily confused as to which direction to take. That was all their pursuers needed to catch up with them, and soon a second furious gunfight broke out in the tunnels. Lazarus and Thompson slammed their backs against a corner while Vasquez and Pahanatuuwa did the same on the opposite side of the corridor.

A bullet whizzed past them and struck a Confederate in the chest. Lazarus looked around. The shot had come from behind them. A figure in a dress swept through the gun smoke like a phantom, the barrel of her long revolver adding to the fug of battle.

Chapter Eighteen

In which our heroes flee to a new future

"Katarina!" cried Lazarus, ecstatic as the Russian flung herself next to him just in time to avoid being hit by the volley of Confederate fire.

"Didn't anyone go topside?" cried Vasquez. "Who's next? Tohotavo and all those other old coots?"

"Just me, bandit," Katarina called back.

"But why?" Lazarus asked her.

"I saw Thompson slip away as we were departing. I don't know what he's planning but I don't trust him. His heart is set on obtaining that gold for the union."

"You were as keen on getting the gold to the union as he is. Have you had a change of heart?"

She shrugged. "I guess somebody taught me that some things matter more than gold."

"Still, the gal's got a point," said Vasquez, eyeing Thompson. "Why did you follow us down here? And don't give me the same bull she did about having second thoughts. From her I might believe it, but you..."

"Vasquez!" cried out a voice from the Confederates before Thompson could answer.

"Reynolds!" Vasquez shouted back.

"It's all over, Vasquez!"

"It ain't over till one of us is dead!"

"You volunteering?"

Vasquez swung around the corner and sent a bullet whizzing towards Reynolds. Three answered in return from different guns, the second striking Vasquez in the thigh. He fell back with a cry of pain. Pahanatuuwa dragged him out of the line of fire.

"Damn him," said Katarina. "Useless heroics…"

"Come on," said Lazarus. "It's pointless to fight here. We need to get to the fuse and get things started. It's the only way to end this."

"Agreed," said Katarina. "You help Pahanatuuwa with Vasquez while I provide covering fire."

She nosed her long revolver around the corner and picked off a Confederate. A hail of fire came their way, and when guns started clicking empty Lazarus and Thompson made a dash to the other side of the passageway.

They struggled to lift Vasquez up onto his good leg. Katarina fired shot after shot, keeping the Confederates on their toes while they half supported, half dragged Vasquez over to her side of the passageway which would lead them onwards.

"They're not following," said Katarina, catching up with them.

"Probably trying to head us off," said Lazarus. "We need to get to the fuse, Pahanatuuwa. Do you know the way?"

The big Cibolan didn't answer but began taking passageways seemingly at random. Lazarus prayed that he knew where he was taking them. They hobbled and stumbled in a northerly direction until they arrived at where they had started, seemingly days ago.

"Light it!" croaked Vasquez.

Lazarus crouched over the fuse and fumbled for

matches while the others covered the passages with their guns.

The click of a revolver sounded loud and close in his ear.

He glanced up and found himself staring down the barrel of Vasquez's pistol, now in the hands of Thompson.

"What the hell are you doing, rebel?" Vasquez cried. "Give me my damned iron back!"

"Can't let you blow this place, Englishman," said Thompson, the gun still pointed at Lazarus's temple.

"I knew it!" said Katarina with a curse. "He planned to sabotage us all along!" She pointed her own revolver at Thompson and cocked the hammer.

"Thompson, think!" said Lazarus. "This is the only way! Reynolds has won otherwise!"

"Not while I still draw breath," Thompson replied.

"You can't win!" said Katarina. "Reynolds will slaughter us all down here and then the gold will be in Confederate hands. Is that really how you want to go out? Is saving the gold really so important that you are willing to let the enemy get it? There is simply no way it can be of any good to you or the union. Perhaps it never was. It doesn't belong to white men, whether they wear gray or blue."

She had walked closer to him now, the barrel of her gun trained on his face, just as his was trained on Lazarus's.

"You don't understand," said Thompson. His voice wavered, cracked under the weight of emotion. "You are just a foreign agent. I have lived with the Confederacy all my life. I have seen what they are capable of. They *must* be stopped at all costs."

"Then keep on fighting them," said Katarina. "*Live.*

Survive this day. *Without* the gold. There will be other chances. Let this gold lie where it is. To try and take it makes us no better than the Confederates who have taken so much from you."

Thompson closed his eyes tight and a single tear rolled down his cheek. His arm relaxed and the gun was lowered. Katarina stepped forward and took it from his grip. He did not resist. She tossed it to Vasquez.

The bandit whistled. "Boy, am I sick of all these standoffs. Let's blow this damned place once and for all!"

Lazarus, fighting down his nerves, returned to his business and eventually got the fuse burning. "Let's get moving!" he said.

"No!" said Katarina. "Listen!"

They listened. Reynolds could be heard barking orders to his men further down the tunnel.

"They're going to try and stop the fuse from reaching the dynamite!" said Lazarus.

"Gotta stop them," groaned Vasquez.

They peered down into the blackness of the tunnel into which the burning end of the fuse had disappeared. It was a no-win situation. To ensure the dynamite would blow, they had to go down there and stop the Confederates from detaching the fuses. But to do that would leave them no time to escape. They did not stop to discuss the matter and followed the sparkling fuse.

They reached the dynamite and began firing upon the Confederates who would have come within seconds of reaching the explosives themselves. Reynolds and his party fell back, taking cover as Lazarus and his companions had done not long before.

"Now what?" asked Katarina. "We can't hang

around here until the fuse reaches the dynamite."

Nobody had a chance to answer, for a second group of Confederates, no doubt come down from the northern temple, were making their way down the passageway towards them. They were trapped between two hostile parties.

"Christ, now we're stuck," said Vasquez, reloading his revolver. "Hok'ee, old pal, I think this is it. I know you have more reason to hate Reynolds than even I do, but I promise you I'll put an extra bullet in him for you. That is, if I have a chance to before the dynamite blows."

"What are you talking about?" Lazarus asked. "You're not suggesting we leave you here!"

"You ain't got a choice," said Vasquez. "My leg won't get me out of here in time, but you three might just make it if you go now. Besides, only one of us needs to remain and guard the fuse. That's gonna be me. Now get going!"

"No!" said Pahanatuuwa.

"Pal, I know. You got more right to kill that bastard than I do, but these three need your gun arm to get them through and up to safety. There's no other way, old buddy."

Lazarus could see the pain in Pahanatuuwa's eyes at the thought of leaving his companion to perish, but even he could see that their choices had been whittled away to this single desperate one.

"Come on, warrior," said Lazarus, putting a hand on the Cibolan's arm. "Your people need you more than Vasquez does."

"And so do we," said Katarina.

"There's just a few more of Reynold's men to kill now," Lazarus added. "And then this valley will be free from them forever."

Pahanatuuwa rose, his eyes fixed on Vasquez.

"Good-bye, Pahanatuuwa," the bandit said, using his birth name for perhaps the first time.

The Cibolan didn't respond. Such was the way of his people who believe that great emotion is expressed best through sullen silence.

"Do you have enough rounds?" Lazarus asked Vasquez.

"I could do with some more, if you're offering."

Lazarus fished out his last two boxes. "One for you and one for me. I hope we both have enough."

"Good-bye, limey. You weren't such a bad fella after all."

Lazarus managed a grim smile. "And neither were you."

"Look after that Russian hussy. She's a wildcat but I kinda like her for it. Just don't turn your back on her…"

"We need to go," said Katarina. "So long, Vasquez. We won't forget this."

Thompson extended his hand. "I have misjudged you it seems, Vasquez," he said. "You would have made a fine partisan."

Vasquez smirked at the idea but took Thomson's hand and shook it all the same.

No more words were spoken, for the fuse was creeping nearer and so were the Confederates on either side. Pahanatuuwa raised his Golgotha and it boomed out, felling the nearest soldier in the party from the north. Time seemed to slow down to treacle as they ran, firing. There was no time to take cover and draw the battle out, only to make a mad charge and hope they could shoot their way through without taking too much damage.

Terrified by the native with the mechanical arm, the Confederates turned tail, but Lazarus and his friends did not stop firing. This was no time for honorable warfare. They shot their enemies in the back, leaping over their fallen forms as they headed on and on towards the northern temple.

They could hear Vasquez shouting behind them, "Come and get it, Reynolds, you fat, crazy bastard!" There was the sound of distant gunfire. Lazarus wiped a tear from his eye as they ran.

The dynamite detonated before they spilled out into the temple complex; an earth-shaking roar that felt like the mountains themselves had been picked up and shaken by some titan. The glittering surface of the last temple they would ever see flashed past their eyes as if it was no more than a fleeting dream.

They could hear the rumble of water behind them as the lake drained into its new basin, filling the tunnels and flooding the rooms of the underground kingdom. They reached the ladder that led up to the kiva and Pahanatuuwa and Thompson scrambled up it, the wood creaking.

"After you," Lazarus said, gripping the ladder.

"Damn English gallantry," Katarina muttered as she hurried up.

At the end of the tunnel he could see the torrent of water thundering towards them like a charging cavalry. He hurried up after Katarina, bumping his head against her rear. She vanished above him, and then he felt Pahanatuuwa's corded arm seize him by the shirt collar and hoist him up into the kiva.

Soon they were out onto the cliff, pounding the red earth with their feet. Behind them, the water erupted out of the kiva like a geyser, lifting its roof many feet into the air before it crumbled and dissolved into muddy rain. The whole cliff edge and its pueblo began to slip and slide down into the valley.

"We need to get higher!" Katarina yelled.

They scrambled up the cliff, scrabbling at the dirt and foliage with their hands, not pausing to look behind them. When they had got as far as they could climb, they found Pahanatuuwa's people staring beyond them from their camp up in the mountain peaks. Only then did they turn around to admire the view.

The whole valley had changed. The shape of the lake was drastically altered and much lower than it had been. All about were fallen trees, mudslides and floating debris. The water that had been tossed into the air drifted about in a spray of mist, causing a fabulous rainbow; a bittersweet contrast to the apocalyptic scene below.

"Good Lord," mumbled Lazarus.

"Did we do the right thing?" Katarina said.

"Ask Pahanatuuwa. I've no idea what's right anymore."

"The kingdom truly belongs to the *kachinas* now," answered the Cibolan. "Not to men, whose greed nearly ruined it. It will lie beneath the lake, forever lost to us. It is a great calamity, but it is right."

"People could still come looking," said Katarina.

"And they won't find it," said Lazarus. "The Seven Golden Cities of Cibola will continue to elude them. And I for one will not mention what I saw here." He looked at her.

"Neither will I," she replied.

They both turned to Thompson. He said nothing

but shook his head and gazed out across the valley.

They were in time for breakfast at the camp in the mountains and ate ravenously while they watched the shifting and settling of the land down in the valley. A group of birds were flocking to a new patch. Nature was adapting to fit its new place, like jelly in a mould.

Pahanatuuwa and Kokoharu approached them. They had been in discussion with the chiefs and elders for most of the morning.

"I have just received confirmation," he said, "that I am to succeed Eototu as chief of the western clan."

"Well congratulations," said Lazarus. "But I thought that to become a chieftain here one had to marry a descendant of the clan's mother?" He then saw Pahanatuuwa's great arm around Kokoharu's middle and knew that he had asked a stupid question. Katarina smirked at him. "Well, I suppose double congratulations are in order."

"Our first child shall be called Vasquez," said Pahanatuuwa somberly.

"Isn't that a rather unusual name for your people?" Katarina asked.

"My people will have to get used to it."

Kokoharu stood up on her tiptoes and kissed her husband-to-be on the cheek. "Together we shall repair the western pueblo and all the other cliff cities," said Pahanatuuwa. "And in time we shall build new cities down in the basin. Each of the seven clans shall have their homes once more. It will be as it has been for generations."

"I wish them all the luck in the world," said Lazarus, as they watched the happy couple walk away to attend to pressing tribal matters.

"As do I," Katarina replied. "But what now? For us,

I mean."

"I think we've outstayed our welcome," Lazarus replied.

"Oh, I don't know. They seem to be preparing for some sort of celebratory feast. I'm sure we're invited."

"Well, I enjoy a tribal feast as much as the next man, but I don't intend to dwell here longer than necessary."

"It's a long walk back to civilization."

"Well, we do know of a dirigible stashed away in an old fort not too many days from here."

She laughed. It was the first time he had ever seen her do so. It pleased him.

"Will you fly it back to London and land it in Trafalgar Square?" she asked.

He chuckled. "I don't think that would make me popular with my government. No, I don't feel quite ready to return to London just yet. I had thought of seeing the eastern cities of the United States. I hear they've more or less rebuilt New York now. You're welcome to join me. Unless you want to take the balloon further, back to Russia."

Her smile faded. "I don't know what will be waiting for me in Russia. A firing squad, perhaps."

"Surely it's not as bad as all that!"

"Perhaps not. But maybe I can put off my return as well." She smiled at him. "We should help Thompson and what's left of his partisan rangers get back to the union. And after all, I've always wanted to see New York."

They sat for a while and watched the birds flapping over the water, winging their way to new lives, finding their paths in the new future thrown up for them by fate.

A Note from the Author

I hope you have enjoyed *Golden Heart*, the first novel in the Lazarus Longman Chronicles. The second novel – *Silver Tomb* – is available for Kindle and in paperback and you can read the first chapter by turning the page!

If you enjoyed *Golden Heart*, you could be very kind and leave a review on Amazon or your retailer of choice, or even just recommend it to somebody. Check out my blog at www.pjthorndyke.wordpress.com where I post about all things Steampunk.

I'm also active on;
Facebook (@PJThorndykeAuthor),
Instagram (pjthorndyke_author)
and Twitter (@PJThorndyke).

Sneak Peek - Silver Tomb

Chapter One

In which our hero is unperturbed by the sound of an exploding horse

As the voices of the muezzins from their minarets carried across the rooftops of the city calling all Mohammedans to *Asr*—the third of the five daily prayers—the heat of the day had barely relented. In his room on the third floor of Shepheard's Hotel, Lazarus Longman listened to the sounds of the Cairo afternoon while he dragged a straight razor across his cheeks and neck, scraping off a mixture of sweat, black bristles and Vinolia Shaving Soap. He carefully avoided the bristles on his top lip, leaving his very neat and very English looking moustache untouched.

He halted as the sound of the explosion echoed down the street below his window and up the walls of the buildings, sending a startled flock of hooded crows flapping and cawing from the roof of a nearby mosque. He held the straight razor frozen an inch from his cheek during the stunned silence that followed the deafening roar, and when the cries of alarm quickly filled the vacuum, he resumed shaving, as uninterested in the racket as he was unsurprised.

He had seen the fools trying to get the iron horse in motion on his way back to the hotel that afternoon. Several *fellahs* had put it into service pulling a cartload of dates. No matter how backward, every country on the globe was trying to imitate the technological leaps and bounds that had been reported and remarked upon in the Confederate and United States of America; a land Lazarus had spent a good deal of time in over the past year. It was true that the streets of American cities were stalked by the iron hooves of steam-powered beasts of burden. Cabs were drawn by remarkable metal contraptions on four legs, belching steam and clanking along with the stuttering and jarring one might expect from a stiff corpse brought back from the dead.

But these were mere pedestrian toys in comparison to the terrifying war machines that continent had dreamed up and put into action in its twenty-five-year-long war. And the countries outside its borders, try as they might, would never even perfect a mechanical donkey without access to the valuable ore known as mechanite which seemed to be unique to the North American continent.

That didn't stop the construction of damn-fool contraptions like the one that had just exploded near Shepheard's Hotel. In the absence of mechanite, the idiots had over-fuelled the coal furnace and let the steam build up to an irresponsible level, resulting in the inevitable explosion. Lazarus had seen this and had tried to warn them, but the fellahs in charge of the contraption had taken his protest as yet another English interference in the Egyptian's natural drive for advancement and had shouted him away. The contraption was a sorry, slapdash affair that would likely have come apart at the rivets before long anyway. They had even put a daft head with ears on the thing that looked like an ironmonger had tried to make a hobby horse for a pantomime.

After his warning had been ignored and he had been rudely ushered on his way, Lazarus had shrugged his shoulders and gone up to the hotel to dress for dinner. He didn't allow his sense of satisfaction at the sound of the mechanical horse exploding draw a smile on his lips. It was bloody dangerous to let simple farmers tinker around with coal furnaces and steam. He didn't doubt that more than one of the fellahs had been scalded in the incident.

He finished shaving and wiped away the residue with a cloth before fixing a collar to his shirt. He went over to the armchair where the morning edition of the *Egyptian Gazette* lay; one of dozens of newspapers printed to cater to the country's large English-speaking population.

He picked it up and rifled through it for the second time that afternoon. There was a report on the continuing investigation into the murder of a renowned Egyptologist whose body had been found scorched and mutilated down at the Bulaq docks. But the main story was the approaching visit of the *CSS Scorpion II*; the gigantic Confederate airship that, stripped of its guns, was crossing the Atlantic and making its way for Cairo on what was, for all Lazarus could gather, a mere show of might.

He scanned the article once more with distaste. The interest of the Confederate States in Egypt and the Suez Canal was worrying. Officially Britain and the C.S.A. were allies, but this landing of the airship in Cairo had the Khedive dancing with glee at the prospect of his British overlord's humiliation. The inevitable overshadowing of their technological and military might by their American cousins, as well as the promise of further foreign investment in his country's fledgling economy would be pleasing to him indeed. The British had held Egypt in a vice of colonialism – however unofficially – ever since they had helped him wrangle the Khedivate back from the nationalist faction of the army and had since showed no signs of loosening their grip.

Now that Her Majesty's empire had its hand in the running of Egypt's economy, it would not take kindly to any American interference in its domination of the trade routes with India. Egypt was not officially part of the empire, but Britain had a financial investment in the improving economy of the country, and had appointed Evelyn Baring, the first Earl of Cromer, as their liaison with the new Khedive.

But allies or not, Lazarus Longman hated the Confederacy with a passion. It had been a gift of fortune that he had escaped from that blasted collection of states with his life, and nothing short of a miracle that he still had a job within the bureau after the debacle of the golden cities of Cibola. But he had bluffed his way through the endless debriefings, bending the truth at times and outright lying at others, and somehow had come out of it unscathed. Now, a year later, he had a different assignment.

Morton had explained the situation to him in his office at Whitehall. He had poured cognac from a decanter into two glasses, muttering irritably as he splashed a fleck on a nearby stack of paperwork.

"It's a missing person's job," Morton said, easing himself down into his chair.

"A bit pedestrian for your office, isn't it?" Lazarus asked. "Why not let the police handle it?"

"It's in Egypt."

"Then why not let the Egyptian police handle it?

The consul has his own special branch there, yes?"

"The Mamur Zapt? Yes, well, it's a little more complicated than that. And I want you specifically to handle it. The case is made for you, or so it seems."

"Oh?"

"You know the party involved, you see."

"Has somebody I know gone missing? I really must keep a closer eye on my acquaintances."

"It's not the missing one you know, but her fiancé."

"Who?"

"Henry Thackeray."

"That pompous arse? Why on earth would I care about his love life, much as it surprises me that he has one."

Morton leveled his eyes at him. "You are not required to *care* about any case beyond your sense of duty to Her Majesty."

"Oh, well played, that, man," Lazarus said in a withering tone. "The old 'duty to the crown' card. It's been at least a year since you used that one on me."

Morton sighed and set down his glass, leaning forward as if the conversation required a more intimate touch. "Look, I know the past few years have been a bloody bad show for you, Longman. I don't blame you if your confidence in the bureau has been shaken. First that bad business in Colombia and then the Cibola washout; it's been a rotten spot of luck. But this affair should be simple enough. A quick job to get you back on your feet, as it were. And your acquaintance with Thackeray isn't the only reason I chose you for the job."

"No? You mean you're handing me this routine plod case because you don't trust me with anything bigger?"

"Not at all. It's Egypt, man! Your area of expertise."

"I have many areas of expertise. Got the diplomas to prove it."

"Among which Egyptology ranks in the first class."

"Tell me, Morton," Lazarus said, "does this missing persons case call much for the reading of hieroglyphics? The ability to place every known pharaoh in his correct dynasty?"

Morton frowned. "Of course not. But you know Cairo. You know the Nile. You probably know every seedy tavern and shady spot better than I dare to guess. And that is what makes you our prime candidate for the job."

"You still haven't said what the job is other than it has something to do with some blower Thackeray has misplaced."

"It's not some blower. Its Eleanor Rousseau, one of France's leading Egyptologists."

Morton had Lazarus's attention now. "I've heard of her. She was one of Mariette's brightest disciples. Knows hieroglyphics better than Champollion did. Thackeray was running around with *her*?"

"Until she went missing. Ordinarily we wouldn't care a fig for a French Egyptologist but it's her relationship with Thackeray that has us worried not to mention the reasons for her sudden disappearing act. He shouldn't have been running around with a French woman, not a man in his position, considering Britain's relationship with France."

"Yes, I hear he's been appointed to the House of Lords."

"Indeed. And his relationship with a French woman was strongly discouraged by the PM and kept hidden from Her Majesty."

"Why on earth did they give him a seat?"

"Lord knows. He's a powerful man and has the type of connections that makes a lowly civil servant like me positively green."

Lazarus smirked. Morton was anything but a 'lowly civil servant' and had connections of his own that were enough to give any man a case of the willies. But still, since Henry Thackeray had come into his inheritance, he was a force to be reckoned with in political circles.

"Whitehall's worried that this French slip of his knows far too much and her disappearance has them in a funk. There are even concerns that she may have maintained a relationship with Thackeray merely to get information from him."

"You mean they think she's a spy?"

"That's one concern."

"An Egyptologist? Funny sort of training for a career as a secret agent…" and then he caught himself. His own career matched that statement exactly and they both knew it. "So, what's the Egyptian connection?"

"That's where she's resurfaced."

"If you know where she is then why am I here?"

"We don't know exactly where in Egypt she is. Her name has come up in Cairo a couple of times and then nothing. It's likely she's out on some dig in the desert. I don't suppose that during your travels in the C.S.A. you ever came across the name Rutherford Lindholm?"

Lazarus shook his head.

"He's an American. From Virginia. A brilliant scientist in the areas of neurology, galvanism and something called 'bio-mechanics'."

As soon as he heard the word Lazarus felt a deep

feeling of unease. "Bio-mechanics?"

"Yes. It's all to do with those ghastly mechanical slaves they build over there. The fusion of the biological with the mechanical. You yourself encountered some of his creations during your time on that continent."

Lazarus suppressed a shudder when he thought of the Mecha-warriors, Mecha-whores and other monstrosities he had witnessed in the Confederate States. He also thought of Hok'ee, or Pahanatuuwa to use his birth name; that gigantic native who had suffered horrific mutilations at the hands of Confederate scientists in their pursuit to perfect a warrior—part man, part machine.

"Professor Lindholm was one of the pioneers of the mechanite revolution, specifically in the creation of mechanical-men. They have organic pilots, you know of course, plugged into steam-powered suits with mechanite furnaces. Bloody unchristian, if you ask me."

"So what does this Lindholm have to do with Eleanor Rousseau?"

"I'm getting to that. It seems that Lindholm has run into difficulties in his homeland. Some sort of legal bother. He's gone rogue, fleeing America and popping up suddenly in Egypt."

"Where he met Rousseau."

"Exactly."

"But why?"

"That's what we want you to find out. Now the C.S.A. are our friends, politically speaking, so ordinarily we wouldn't touch him. But if he's gone rogue…"

"Then we can grab him and squeeze him for secrets. I just don't see the Rousseau connection."

"Neither do we, but they've been seen together, and she has written to her fiancé—ex- fiancé, I should imagine by now—that she was embarking on a dig with an eminent American scientist, although she didn't mention his name. We don't know what his interest in Egyptology is, and quite frankly the whole business has us stumped. Shortly after Rousseau's letter to Thackeray, all correspondence stopped. He even went over there to find her, but all traces of her have vanished. He's worried that she may be romantically involved with Lindholm."

Lazarus snorted with mirth.

"The poor bugger's frantic. Reuniting the two isn't in our interests of course but bringing her back to Blighty is top priority. National safety aside, it could avoid a very nasty scandal; House of Lords member bedding a French spy, that sort of thing. And the more you find out about this Lindholm, the better. It's probably just a nasty bit of sordidness, you know how these French are. Still, worth a look."